THE LAST NEWS VENDOR

The publication of *The Last News Vendor* has been generously supported by the Canada Council for the Arts and the Ontario Arts Council.

Editor: Luciano Lacobelli
Typography & Cover Design © 2019, Jared Shapiro

Library and Archives Canada Cataloguing in Publication

Title: The last news vendor / Michael Mirolla.
Names: Mirolla, Michael, 1948- author.
Identifiers: Canadiana 20190166150 | ISBN 9781988254715 (softcover)
Classification: LCC PS8576.I76 L37 2019 | DDC C813/.54‚Äîdc23

Published by Quattro Books Inc.
Toronto, Canada
www.quattrobooks.ca

Printed in Canada

THE LAST NEWS VENDOR

Michael Mirolla

QUATTRO BOOKS

The **newsvendor model** is a mathematical model in operations management and applied economics used to determine optimal inventory levels. It is (typically) characterized by fixed prices and uncertain demand for a perishable product. If the inventory level is q, each unit of demand above q is lost in potential sales. This model is known as the *newsvendor problem* by analogy with the situation faced by a newspaper vendor who must decide how many copies of the day's paper to stock in the face of uncertain demand and knowing that unsold copies will be worthless at the end of the day.

—Wikipedia

for Jackie and all the gang

A: Prelude To Any Action

or

Notes of Delphic Importance

I.

After thirteen days of having intensely studied Sully (or Cully) and his newsstand, both through close at hand observation and by means of a pair of army surplus 8 X 40 binoculars, I am now (or was then?) able to surface with this series of descriptions, notes, and reflections—not to mention the premises, assumptions and conclusions needed as a necessary prelude to any meaningful action:

Notes On The Behaviour of Cully (Or Sully),
The News Vendor, As Diligently Compiled
Between March Eighth and Twentieth

1. His name is Arthur Sully (or Cully), I can't be sure which. That's because the hand-painted wooden sign over his newsstand reads either: 'ARTHUR SULLY'S NEWS-A-RAMA' or 'ARTHUR CULLY'S NEWS-A-RAMA', with the 'S' and the 'C' superimposed one on the other. It may have been a slip of the sign-designer's brush and a half-hearted attempt at correcting it. Or his predecessor might have been Cully and he Sully. Or the opposite. Or he might have simply changed his last name. Or he may have left the previous owner's name on the sign. Whatever. I probably coul• fin• out for sure on closer inspection. But it •oesn't really make much of a •ifference to me—at least not at this point. I'll just refer to him as the News Vendor. Is he the last News Vendor left? In this city, most likely. I can't speak for other places. Perhaps there are still some for nostalgia's sake in cities like London and Paris. But in this particular city, I have not run across any others. And I've roamed up and •own its streets—from mountain (both cis- an• trans-) to sea, from forest to skyscraper. Assumption: having opted for pixels on screens of all sizes, and devices that are friendly and respond nonjudgmentally to the most awkward of personal questions including bowel movements, the public for the most part has stopped purchasing paper news. It's so retro, as my daughter likes to say. Or in the words of my partner: Why bother with all that searching when the search comes to you with a couple of clicks? Or voice request?

2. *The Newsstand: It may be dilapidated. It may be falling apart. It may have holes through which the wind can whistle. It may be in need of several coats of paint, right now a faded army green. But it is nevertheless a thing of beauty. Something that deserves to be preserved. A hexagonal over-hanging roof provides both shade and some protection from the weather. Across the front, a window swings out horizontally and is pinned back to reveal all the treasures within. To one side, a door that can be opened both fully or only the top half with shelving exposed when open; on the other, a series of slats that slide away an• allow potential customers to enter. It's a mo•el of efficiency with every nook and cranny packed with objects of pleasure if not pure knowledge. How could you not but admire ...? I'm getting ahead of myself. Stick to observations, please.*

3. *The News Vendor: He's old. Extremely old. So old that ... Hmmm, that might prove the first •ifficulty. No, no. Think improvisation. A touch of suffering— an• there'll be plenty of that, I'm sure—an• a matter of time, that's all. A matter of time. The wrinkles, the lines, all the troubling marks and symbols of age will come. Simply a matter of time.*

4. *He's bald. No comment. Well, maybe just one comment. He's not exactly or completely bald. A curly silver fringe, like steel wool, sticking out around the ears and back of neck. Anyway, not to worry. The crown of his head is usually covered by a greasy blue-grey sailor's cap and can be seen only when he removes that cap to wipe his brow.*

5. *He possesses only one leg. He ... —Only one leg! Christ on a stick! Only one leg! I mean only one real leg, one leg of flesh an• bone—an• that itself being mostly bone. The other's wooden, a peg-leg of the antique pirate type, slightly warped and cracked with age, which he straps on with leather thongs. Many marks and holes in it. As if he has been jabbing old-style compasses or pen-knives into it to whittle away the time. On the other hand, it might only be the work of termites after all. Busy little insects missed by the housing inspector. Able to create mounds that can be seen from outer space. And having found a perfect place to both hide and feed amid all that pulp and paper.*

6. *Dress: A red –*

—

One of my children, the youngest a boy I think (and name withheld to protect the truly innocent), waddles into the study-cum-bedroom at this moment and demands I help him open the door to the washroom. It's stuck, he says, eyes shut tight, wiggling back and forth and crossing his legs like scissors. I stop pounding on my typewriter—yes, a typewriter, I'm not ashamed to admit—and follow him out to the bathroom. The door isn't stuck. His sister, the adolescent one I think (name withheld to protect the not so innocent), is at full gallop, ripping blackheads from her face. She refuses to open the door and I refuse to threaten her into complying. Instead, I prepare an extemporaneous chamber pot (a large orange juice tumbler actually) and he relieves himself, sighing all the while. Thanks, dad, he says when it is over. You're the greatest. I nod proudly but he's already back to his Laugh & Learn Smart Stages Laptop.

I am just about to turn and head back into my room to continue the "Notes" when my partner—best to also leave her nameless in case there are reprisals against me—bursts through the front door all out of breath and reeking of excitement. You wouldn't believe it, she says, simultaneously throwing her purse and coat on to the sofa, pecking me on the cheek and then turning towards the flickering TV image in the corner, a daytime talk show/reality TV/self-help/bailiff's court amalgam for those who do not have time to take in each of these programs separately. Someone tried to assault one of the girls outside the club last night, she continues, plunking herself down on the sofa, in the exact spot just recently abandoned by my daughter before her blackhead crisis. I ask if she'd been hurt and my partner laughs. Hurt! Why, she sucked the little weenie wimp dry and then sent him stumbling on his way, offering him her black panties as a commemorative of the occasion.

A muffled cell phone rings, a Unit 9 ringtone, I've been told. Whatever that means as I don't own a cell phone. My partner fishes through her purse, settles back on the sofa, crosses her legs and begins an animated conversation, filled with OMGs and LOLs. I shut the door behind me and sit once more at the typewriter. It is a typewriter and not a laptop. And not just any typewriter either but an Underwood Mod. 3, handed down to me from my grandfather who often called himself the last of the true newspapermen. Always "newspapermen" rather than "newspaperpersons" or "newspaperpeople". Depending on his state of inebriation, he originally got the typewriter either from Ernest Hemingway or Jack Kerouac. And either as a result of a poker game or having helped Ernest and/ or Jack put the finishing and definitive touches to their novels while simultaneously translating either Sartre's plays or Kafka's unfinished short stories.

—

March 22nd

Continuation of The Notes
From The Previous Day

6. *Dress: A red-and-green checkered shirt, rough wool, of the kind used by deer hunters. Worn out and threadbare around the collar and left elbow, with several buttons missing. Always the same one which he washes in the evening and hangs out to dry. Or maybe he rotates several identical ones. Baggy brown pants, very thin and shiny at the knees, which billow out with the slightest win•—both internal an• external. The impression of the twin bones of his buttocks can be seen clearly when the breeze is behind him. The pants, made for a man twice his size and usually rolle• up to his knees—to emphasize the peg-leg, no •oubt, in an effort to elicit sympathy—are hel• up by a fraye• but shiny yellow cor•. Piece of shielded electrical wire, maybe, and coded for wattage/amperage but of no great significance as I •oubt most woul• notice a variation in either colour or composition.*

7. *Domicile: He lives on the secon• floor of a three-story hotel •irectly across from his newsstand and in a room that looks down on it. The hotel, like him, is windswept and seedy. Pockmarked and rattling. With the traditional on an• off vertical neon sign—the type that remin•s me of Elvis for some reason—whimsical in its lighting. In fact, with rooms rente• out by the week and to more or less permanent tenants, it's more like a slum boarding house than a real hotel. I've watched him through my reliable binoculars for the past thirteen days as he sits in front of the window in a creaky rocking chair after removing his wooden leg. He leans heavily on the leg, using it as an awkwar• cane—with one en• against the window-sill and the other under his chin. He never takes his eyes from the sealed and locked newsstand (lit up all night by a nearby moth-splattered street lamp) until I imagine their li•s shut •own on their own into fitful*

sleep. But, even with eyes shut, he tenses and stops rocking the moment anyone lingers near the stand. As if he's already experienced some terrible calamity in connection with it. Or expects to in the near future. He even jumped up one day last week when a prostitute stopped in front of it, using the light to fix her make-up an• to wipe a mascara'• tear from her eye. I say "her" but it could just as easily have been a "him" given the popularity of drag in this part of town. The News Vendor was half-way into strapping his leg back on when she move• off again an• he fell back into his chair. As far as I can tell from my vantage point, the room itself is almost completely empty with not a single sign of any modern conveniences. No computer, TV, telephone, radio ... I approve. I approve wholeheartedly. Distractions are called that for a reason. Extreme concentration is of the essence for any significant task, is it not?

8. *Disposal: Other news vendors (lower case) return (or used to return when they still existe•) unsol• papers an• magazines to their suppliers—so they don't have to pay for those they haven't been able to sell. Have a weekly or monthly pick-up or something like that. Not him. Nor does he believe in the postmodern mantra of recycling/reworking/reusing. Once a week, he gathers up the leftovers and places them in a large burlap sack with the name "Jean-Louis Lebris" on the side. Then he drags this sack down to the arm of the river—a •elta or bay really—that exten•s in just beyon• the railroa• tracks. Once there, he pulls a small boat out of the shadows, rows out and dumps the sack into the brackish waters.*

9. *In the morning –*

—

My partner chooses this particular moment to again interrupt. Massaging each of her breasts very carefully in front of the full-length bedroom mirror—a gift from an anonymous admirer (the mirror, that is; she is paying for the breasts herself on an instalment plan)—and rubbing them with special oil that makes them glisten with good health, she wants to know if I planned on sleeping with her again or if I'll be spending the rest of my nights in the alleys. I try to explain that this was typical exaggeration on her part, that I didn't spend my nights in alleys but rather on perfectly respectable and well-lit streets. Also that, from this day forward, I'd make it a point to be home more often, at least at night.

She pretends to understand but she doesn't really—and I don't expect her to. I mean, who does? I leave her to massage those expensive breasts in front of the mirror. This practice mustn't be taken for misplaced vanity on her part. Or an effort at sexual stimulation to revive what looks, from the outside, like a flagging relationship. No, breast massage is an important element in her work preparation. As arguably an artiste's most valuable assets, they must always be firm, must not ever sag due to lack of attention or inexcusable absentmindedness. And a certain level of enhancement always helps. As is aiming for perfection. Smiling, I turn over and go to sleep, resolving to continue my "Notes" on my favourite park bench tomorrow where my chances of being interrupted are much less. Although it means I have to write them out by hand rather than on the typewriter and then transcribe them later.

—

March 23rd

Continuation of The Notes—Part Two

9. *In the morning, he crosses the street, making his way through the heavy traffic on Julius Street without ever once looking where he's going. As if he has some special immunity that causes the cars to skirt around him. Or maybe it's a built-in magnetic pole to repel any vehicle that comes too close. Then he proceeds to carry out the ritual of opening his newsstand. I call it a "ritual" because it is never altered. Not in the least detail. Or, at any rate, it hasn't been for the thirteen days I've had him under observation. He checks the small space behind the newsstand, the less than one foot separating it from the stern windowless grey stone jail-like building (with 'Rabensteiner, Kullich and Kaminer, Attorneys At Law' chiselled across the studded metal door) in front of which it sits—like a piece from a multi-coloure▪ Mi▪▪le Eastern bazaar. I assume he checks this space between building and stand for any scraps of paper or other foreign objects that may have lodged there during the night. Or perhaps he fears a very thin, very agile thief waiting to pounce as he opens his stand. Six days of the week, he circles the newsstand twice, once clockwise and then back counter-clockwise; on Sundays, this is reverse▪. He checks behin▪ it again, always fin▪ing something new, either*

because he didn't bother removing it the first time or else because he put it there himself on his clockwise circling. He mumbles as he fits the wrong key into the lock (he has two on his chain). He shakes his head, looks left then right, as the second key slides smoothly in. He opens it with dramatic flair, throwing back the door in almost operatic fashion. Finally, he hauls in the bundles of newspapers and magazines which I assume are left overnight by his suppliers (with a piece of paper at the top that reads: 'Schloss Distributors'), bundles which appear to be getting smaller by the day. Once inside, he throws open the front window and slides the slats to one side. Except on Sundays, of course, when he remains closed and thus carries out the ritual only to the mumbling and the wrong key.

10. *Before he spreads out the day's papers and begins to sell in earnest, he makes several early customers wait as he slowly removes his wooden leg (a simple matter, really, of unstrapping it from his stump) and places it in a conspicuous position against the opened slats, just beneath the comics. There it remains all day, bleaching in the sun, warping in the rain. Around the newsstand, he's as agile on one leg as on two, hopping about like a flamingo or a kangaroo and using the various hooks strewn above his head as supports. As if on a bus or tram. I've yet to see him fall. Correction on that: He did fall once but I'm not sure it counts. It happened when a customer changed her mind about buying a stack of magazines. The News Vendor suddenly collapsed to the filthy floor, invalid and helpless and oh so pathetic as he flailed his arms. After being helped up, he sold the customer not only the original stack of magazines but several day-old newspapers and a* News of The World *as well.*

—

A woman at the other end of the park bench with sand-filled garbage bags tied around her waist keeps staring at me and nodding in my direction. It is as if she knows me or at the very least wishes to make my acquaintance. I nod back and even try waving at her. Discreetly, of course. As nothing is more embarrassing than waving or smiling at someone and not getting anything back for it. But that's before I discover she really doesn't know me. And, in fact, she isn't actually staring at me or nodding in my direction because … well, because … to be blunt about it … she is blind. Utterly and without a doubt.

She talks on in a disjointed way to no one in particular, to the air around her really. When she isn't talking, she giggles and slaps her thighs and picks her nose, rubbing its contents between thumb and forefinger before flicking them into the air. As she talks (and she starts just about every conversation with: "Call me anything but don't call me Winnie"), she bobs her head in counter beat to her speech patterns. Like Ray Charles or something. No one else has ever paid any attention to her although she is constantly calling out names, making reference to relationships, gesturing for people to stop and listen. For what she has to say, so she says, is important to their survival. Of extreme importance. But no one listens. No one bothers to stop. In fact, they speed up or cross the street to get out of what soon becomes shouting range as quickly as possible. And do you blame them? Would you stop to listen to a blind woman leaving a trail of sand and dried snot behind her?

So she talks on and on and she strokes a wispy white beard (a string of loose hairs really dangling from her chin) where the dribble and bread crumbs gather and she tugs on her curly hair as if she wants to yank it out and she makes fists and she does a two-step shuffle that sounds like Fred Astaire and she grinds her rotting teeth. Spitting out the stubs. Well, it seems that way anyway. But in truth these are pieces of semi-masticated noodles. All grist for the mill.

—

Same Day Continuation—Part Three

11. *It would seem logical for the News Vendor to simply reverse the ritual at night when he must close ♦own—starting from the locking of the ♦oor an♦ working his way back to checking the space behind the stand. But logic doesn't enter into it and he does it in exactly the same way as in the morning. It's performed with an air of dejection, however, with none of the vigour or enthusiasm of the opening. As if there's nothing else to look forward to, nothing outside the newsstand, neither diversion nor passion. And there doesn't seem to be—at least not for him. I can't for the life of me figure out why the ritual is so important though. Perhaps it creates a force-fiel♦ or gravity well. Something that anchors the stand, that prevents it from suddenly lifting up on its haunches an♦ slinking off with the ven♦or's newspapers into someone else's domain. Like on some magic carpet. But I've walked by it several times an♦ haven't felt a thing—not even the least tug or warping. Simply a ♦ilapi-*

dated box around the corner from a scummy alley on the edge of a scummier swamp.

12. *Amendment to observation (3). He's not that old, not really that old at all. Just seems that way. An attempt at sympathy perhaps. Or so that anyone stealing from him will acquire a guilty conscience along with a stack of papers. Both useless, of course—one in the short, one in the long run. Anyway, what looke•d from afar like deep wrinkles across his forehead turn out to be scars, symmetrical markings like those of a Zulu warrior. Or Maori islander.*

13. *Peculiar. I've just walke•d up an•d bought my first paper from him (this being March 20th). Most peculiar. No pictures of nu•de women—with their legs sprea•d an•d •dark strategic X's slashe•d across pubic hair an•d anal openings— line the interior of his stand as they do the others I'd visited in my youth. Nor does he sell magazines of this type, not even the lucrative brown-bagged ones direct from Sweden (for cachet purposes but actually from Hollywood these days) that vie for space next to* Captain America. *What does he sell then? The few remaining dailies, of course, from the politically correct to the racially motivated. Weekly tabloids obviously with twin-headed Presidents being controlle•d by aliens or KGB foreign governments in •devil outfits. An•d the glossies, beaming with Reality TV guest hosts and cover girls. But the largest proportion of what he sells consists of romance magazines, period piece magazines, large-caption picture magazines fille•d with •dreamy-eye•d women reaching out towards the unknown, towards the captains of their fate, the tall, dark shapers of their destinies. A personal preference or an astute economic decision?*

14. *His eyes are a washed-out grey (contact lenses?). When there are no customers (and this means for a good part of the day), he spends his time sitting on a small stool, reading. What he reads I haven't been able to discover. He doesn't read what he sells. Of that I'm sure. His own reading material comes from a small chamber behind him, a padlocked chamber, and is kept out of sight beneath the counter. He guards this reading material jealously, quickly hiding it when a customer appears.*

II.

Notes On The Very First Day
of Observation: March 8th

There's a mole on my partner's left breast, just above the nipple and a little to the outside of the aureole. A tuft of hair encircles this mole. It's a tuft of thin golden hair, wispy and practically see-through. One must get quite close to spot it and then, as the breast swells before your eyes, it glistens in the proper light. I've known this ever since those first hea•y •ays when, as teenagers in wet-trouser love, we'd slip away into cool but dusty basements where the old, springless mattresses were stored. And we'd remove our clothes in ceremonial slow motion and lie down next to each other and just stare at the miracle, the uncorrupte• flesh.

But I'm told of the mole anew this morning by a stuttering, cross-eyed regular at the Absinthe A-Go-Go. He says he's been observing the thing for several •ays now as my partner comes off the stage after her performance, comes down among the customers to serve drinks and chit-chat. He's thinking, he says as he winks and elbows me in the ribs, of making it his life study. He knows it's a real mole and not one of those pasted on fakes because it grows more hairy as he grows more drunk. And it doesn't shift positions like the one on the left buttock of the other girl. Also, he says in an ingenious non sequitur, he knows a trick guaranteed to harden the nipples on even the most inured of prostitutes and would I like to know what it is. I nod.

"Just b ... b ... blow on them. Cool them off an• watch them stiffen. That's all there's to it. They can't help themselves. Let me show you."

He calls one of the girls over and demonstrates successfully on her. Then tells me to give it a try, to prove it isn't just some chemical in his breath that does it. I'm leaning towards her about to blow gently when my partner comes over. I suck in my breath and grin. The drunk man loosens his tie and begins to blow at my partner's breasts, his eyes able to track both at once as they jiggle in front of him. She stands there disdainfully for a moment, scratching her belly button, and then turns away.

"Stiff c ... c ... cunt," he stutters. "Only one reme•y for a stiff cunt."

"What's that?" I ask, ever anxious to learn.

"I know another tr ... tr ... trick ..."

He reaches into his pocket and pulls out a wad of bills. I smile at him, at the girl waiting with her hand out for his latest trick, at my partner's back, at him again. And then leave. I think I've seen this trick before.

Although my partner has given me specific or•ers not to visit her •uring working hours, claiming my presence disturbs her concentration and makes her feel self-conscious, thus costing her tips especially when she's doing pelvic rotations on the tables, I invariably fin• myself mean•ering to the club. What else is there to do? My partner earns enough for both of us and I've no interest in a job. The chil•ren are well taken care of—one at the nursery; the other in regular school. In short, I've no obligations and so am free to wander about the city. A flâneur, I tell myself—an• •on't you forget the circumflex over the "a".

Yet, no matter how far away I begin the •ay—sometimes I borrow a bit of money and ride the bus all the way to the riverfront or up into the mountains or •own to the beaches—I always en• up working my way back to the centre of town. Back to these two or three blocks of hotels, clubs, pool halls, department and surplus stores, tourist rooms and church, a single solitary Gothic-style church. I know the area inside out. I've heard every classical album (no CDs, thank you very much) found in the sound shops. The toilets in the hotels have my name enshrined in plastic until the next paint job. I've smuggled not a small number of books from the second-hand dealers, using them to line the inside of my jacket and even as jock-straps when I've no other place to put them.

At first, I believe• it was because of my partner that I always spiralle• my way here, sideways from back-alley to back-alley like a crab. It was only natural. After all, memory is a powerful and prickly thing and the memory of warm flesh even more so. But for some time, I've suspecte• this was merely a useful camouflage for the true reason, for the real attraction. To•ay, as that drunk loosened his tie and told me about the real mole surrounded by a tuft of real hair, I suddenly realized it wasn't my partner who drew me to this area. Not her at all. May perhaps have been her once in a time of dusty basements an• springless mattresses an• virgin flesh but not any more. It was rather the News Vendor. For several years, I've been walking through this particular block of Julius Street, past the beggar with his felt-marker-on-cardboard The Hungry Artist sign, and by the newsstand without noticing *the News Vendor properly, without noticing even the wooden leg as it leaned against a corner of the stand. I guess it must have been a great man who said the first thing we overlook is the obvious.*

—

To call the realization a sudden one and an overlooking of the obvious is an unnecessary joke of mine which I thought amusing at the time. I'd known all along what I was after and why I was drawn to the area. It's just that I had developed the habit of establishing decoys along the way so that the hunters would have more trouble finding me. Decoys such as partner, daughter, son, beggar, and so forth. So ingrained is the habit that I find myself doing it even now when it's no longer needed and leads only to confusion for myself. Besides, I now know the ploy is useless. A waste of energy and time. The hunters, if persistent, need only follow the decoys to sooner or later flush me out. Or they can set out decoys of their own and totally confuse me and my decoys. Decoying the decoy.

—

Notes On Night-Time Activity: March 11th

There he is as I bring him close-up and into focus, propped up on left elbow in his greasy window and rubbing his chin. As if that simple rubbing is all that's needed to erase the day's growth of stubble. And maybe it is, for he always emerges clean-shaven in the morning. The flowers on the window-sill (in the vase that resembles the bottom-half of a Javel bottle) are undeniably plastic and made to match the printed ones on the curtains and wallpaper. I've a similar bouquet at home—of a different colour but equally unnatural. No, I'm in error. His are real. Just made to look plastic to fool the bees. Bees? There are no bees here. Where would one expect to find bees on a busy down-town street? I know they're real because he's watering them, feeding them from a glass whose edges are covered with dried toothpaste in the form of lip impressions. Wait a minute. That doesn't prevent the flowers from being plastic. Of course, it doesn't. How stupid of me. Perhaps he only waters them so that the earthworms and dung beetles and potato bugs can drink as I'm sure they get little nourishment from the roots of plastic flowers—no matter how long-lasting those flowers tend to be.

If I stare long enough, that glass, now only half-fille♦ with water, will float to his lips of its own accor♦, will part them an♦ force the liqui♦ ♦own his throat. He'll remove the wooden leg from under his chin so that he may guzzle in peace and then he'll replace it in the exact same position. So unreal is this sequence of events that only by witnessing it can I prove—to myself at least—that it actually took place, that he really move♦ at all. During the two nights I've observed him (not including this evening as yet), I've seen him move from the window only for this guzzling and the feeding of his pseu♦o-plastic flowers. He sleeps for perio♦s of a few minutes—at the most. Then wakes again, his eyes snapping open with undisguised fear, with the look of a man who has lost something during the short time they've been shut.

—

During my vigils, I am able to stay awake and alert only because I sleep on alternate days and nights. For example: March eighth, I was awake day and night. March ninth, I slept all day but was awake at night. March tenth, awake all day but slept at night. March eleventh, awake all day and night. Etc. It is all calculated in my plan. Well, maybe not from the very beginning but at least as I went along, solidifying in the actual doing of it. And I include it here to give an air of credibility to my task so that none may say I omitted the basic realities, that's it all merely a flight of fancy with no concern for that animal part of ourselves that requires nourishment and rest. And visits to the boys' room. At first, I thought it was regretful on my part that I didn't have a camera with which to record my observations. Or at least what passes for a camera these days stuffed into the guts of so-called smart phones. It might have been the final proof I needed to assure myself of what I was doing. On the other hand, the ability of memory and imagination to surpass and even supplant basic realities made them much more important tools than any camera or smart phone. Besides, one must have a little distortion to keep the perspective clear.

—

Continued Notes on Night-Time Activity: March 11th

A woman comes towards me, swollen in size by the binoculars. She disappears against the angular shadows of the buildings and then re-appears beneath the domes of the street-lights. She stops and smiles at me. I hold out a twenty-dollar bill and ask her if she can do me a favour. Sure, sailor, she says, moving towards me. No, I say, here's what I want you to do. And I ask her to fix her make-up an• preten• to wipe a tear from her eyes in front of the newsstand. In front of what? In front of the newsstand?

She looks around for the newsstand. Yes, I say, the place that sells newspapers. She stares at me blankly, as if she hasn't understood a thing, though they are the simplest words possible. I don't understand, she says. I lean closer, fighting off the perfume an• the o•our of something else that struggles to come through. I repeat the instructions, waving the money before her eyes. She follows the bill for several seconds, then grabs it and continues to stare at me until I push her off, telling her she'll get another twenty upon completion of her easy task.

She begins to walk again, swaying, till she gets to the newsstand. She stops and, after looking back at me once more, slowly, languidly wipes the corners of her lips and eyes. The light turns her into a pale mannequin, something just escaped from a store window and now hoping through some act or gesture or combination of both to become human. I expect any moment for her to tire of the game an• to go in the other •irection—to begin peeling away her eye-brows, her hair, her ears, her breasts, her belly button ... to emerge as an experimental android set out amid humans to determine if AI can go undetected commingling with the general population.

The News Vendor in his greasy window uncoils from the rocking chair. And, though it's too dark to see, even with binoculars, I can easily imagine his face pushing harshly against the window pane, inadvertently cleaning portions of it. And looking suddenly younger as it's distorted by the window, the scars ... markings ... tattoos ... flattene• an• erase•. I can imagine his nose, squashed, widening to reveal the thick hairs in his nostrils. And fogging the glass with his frantic breathing. Not to mention his eyes bulging to the point of popping out.

The woman ... the android fashionably sexless ... turns to look back at me. I give her/it the thumbs up sign and wave her/it on, having learned all that I nee•e• to know. She/it hikes her/its mini-skirt so that white flesh is visible along the top of her/its black mesh stockings and moves back towards me as she/it had entered, disappearing against the square shadows of build-ings and then re-appearing beneath the canopy of streetlights. I hand her/ it the other twenty as she/it slides by. You've passed the test, I whisper. At least I can't tell the •ifference. The News Ven•or collapses in his chair. That I can see. But that he's breathing with •ifficulty an• hol•ing his chest is only supposition. As is the jabbing of a finger into his mouth to help bring up a meal that seems to be stuck half-way between his throat and his stomach.

—

My partner has tried many potions and chants—potions and chants she claims to get through what she calls "Google" searches—in an effort to make herself more attractive to me during these last few weeks before I leave for good. She feels it is somehow her fault that I'd rather walk the streets at night than be in bed with her, especially since our relationship has been exemplary till now. I explain as best I can that it has nothing to do with her and, to prove it, make a gallant effort to respond to her. But to no avail. My heart isn't in it. She would hold me tight, so tight I had on occasion to pry her fin-gers loose. When that doesn't work, she goes back to drinking her mixtures and reciting incantations. And so, during the times when I do stay home, I would hear her whispering cryptic words that make little sense while holding boiling, bubbling concoctions in mason jars and lifting them skyward:

The man of Ea am I,
The man of Damkina am I,
The messenger of Marduk am I,
My spell is the spell of Ea,
My incantation is the incantation of Marduk,
The circle of Ea is in my hand,
The tamarisk, the powerful weapon of Anu,
In my hand I hold,
The •ate—spathe, mighty in •ecision,
In my hand I hold.

The smell of her potions isn't as nauseous as the ingredients would lead one to believe: powdered frogs' legs, peanut butter jelly, a pinch of calcium chloride, chopped crab grass, and a spider or two (if available). All stirred with a beaver tail and under strict instructions never to change the direction of the stirring. Despite the lack of smell, it is still unpleasant to watch her hold her nose and gulp this down and I shudder every time, making sure to cover the children's eyes. On what will be my last day at home, she has a new, more ominous incantation:

He who forges the image, he who enchants –
The spiteful face, the evil eye,
The mischievous mouth, the mischievous tongue,
The mischievous lips, the mischievous words,
Spirit of the Sky, remember!
Spirit of the Earth, remember!

She recites this while holding an iPad with one hand and a wrinkled lemon over the gas range with the other. The lemon is studded with nails whose tips are starting to glow. But not from the heat as the elements have not yet been lighted.

—

Notes on A Sunday: March 14th

It's seven-thirty in the a.m. on a Sunday morning and he's pacing in front of his stand after going through the ceremony of almost opening it. There's no one else visible on the street (at this moment), although it's possible someone might come into view just like that, rounding a corner or slipping drunkenly out of an alley. He paces furiously, as if he were on the quarter-deck of an ancient wooden sailing ship, shouting orders down at the crew, snarling at the incompetence of the crow's nest for not spotting the trouble sooner, impaling the first mate's mutiny on the tip of a curry-•ippe• swor•. Or perhaps his sharpened tongue.

There's a bir• that whispers secrets in his ear, a bir• that floats high above the world and knows everything. The bird's nestled beneath an oversized yellow raincoat which drags the ground each time he comes down on his wooden leg. It's raining. It's raining and I'm left to speculate where he'll go now that he has nothing to do because it's Sunday and he refuses absolutely to sell papers on Sunday. The pool hall, of course. Where else? The pool hall, with its green velvet tables and long sticks and coloured balls with numbers.

I follow him to the pool hall and watch him shoot a few games. He uses his wooden leg instead of a cue, rubs the front of it with chalk, leans over the table, his good leg securely on the ground. The others are hypnotized into losing, into believing they, too, hold wooden legs in their hands, too thick and bulky to handle properly. Or maybe real legs with the blood not yet dry on them, their owners the true victims of my partner's rituals.

A bell claps an• thu•s, muffle• by a scarf of rain. He's still pacing, still pacing, hasn't gone anywhere. Then suddenly he begins to walk towards me, looming larger an• larger, his coat flapping open to reveal a large yellow bird. Past me now, his body becoming one motion in the rain, one compli-cated motion that has taken a lifetime to perfect itself: slight forward jerk, then up, then down with a slight forward jerk and a sideways slip to main-tain absolute balance. Beautiful. I swell up with pride at my choice. What a beautiful limp. Precious. The most precious thing he has. And he knows it. Knows it so well.

This time he'll turn into the pool hall. For sure. Watch this. Nope. Past the pool hall. The penny arcade, then. Do they still call it that? Whatever. Call it the spirit of the penny arcade. He's a natural penny arcade man, hovering over the games like a malignant spirit. Or getting right in there among the controls. Morphing into the penny dreadful maybe. Nope. Past the penny arcade. Past the … Up-step; down-step; sideways slip; up-step. Christ, it's the church. He's going into the church. Will they allow him in? Are church-going pirates allowe•? The sign on the front says: To•ay's Sermon—The Grimoire of Pope Honorius.

I finger the me•allion aroun• my neck which guarantees I won't •ie without a priest at my side, without a benediction to secure my place in Purgatory—which, un•er the circumstances, is the best I can hope for. He has entered it now. He has actually entered the church without once being stopped, without once being asked to prove he believes, to show his faith, to renounce the yellow bird. I hover outside, nervous, my right eye-lid twitch-ing. Trying to decide. Knowing I'll be stopped if I go in. Bracing myself for the righteous blast that will blow him out again—an• me right behin• him.

It doesn't come. And then I bound up as well, my gait becoming slower an• slower as I reach the top of the steps. The church is completely fille•. Packe• to the rafters. Only one hea• turns—that of an ol• woman with a moustache an• spike-like hairs on her chin—as the soun• of rain enters with me and then is left behind again. The chorus lifts a joyous refrain over the bowed heads of the people: Ad Deum qui laetificat juventutem meam. A High Mass! The full liturgical treatment with no holds barred. The glitter and the splendour. No wonder it's packed.

I'm looking for the Vendor. Where might he be? My hands are trembling as I stand at the back. There's a huge chandelier swinging delicately over my head. When I was forced to go to church regularly in my youth, I spent a lot of time trying to calculate the probability of one of those chandeliers falling in the midst of atoning heads. To crush them. Or slice them off at the neck, cleanly if a little jaggedly. At the very least selecting the hypocrites for special treatment. I often contemplated doing it myself—leaping up from the choir loft to the top of the chandelier and forcing it down with my added weight. But I feared the priest had an automatic rifle hidden beneath his pulpit and would immediately pick me off as a devil incarnate. (They have licence and a general dispensation to do such things—the Church's version of the Second Amendment.)

Besides, the people with no heads would go on praying anyway if they had any faith at all. They would, I tell you. Where's that Vendor? An old woman—the same old woman who turned to watch me enter—suddenly clutches her stomach and rushes out. Punished for not paying close enough attention, for turning at the wrong moment. A tough task master. I take her seat. It's warm. I try to do what everyone else does but kneeling is a problem. I can't kneel. Nothing psychological. Not at all. My mind is willing but my knees just won't bend. I compromise and remain half-seated at the edge of the pew.

At last, just as I'm about to give up, I spot the Vendor a few rows in front of me, a gleam of light from the chandelier polishing his bald pate (now that he's removed his sailor's cap). He's quiet, taciturn, head bowed, pensive, not singing. He turns sideways to shush a fidgety child. Wait. Wait. That's not him. How could I have ever imagined that incorrigible grandfather to be the Vendor? No, no. There he is, further down, singing lustily, a yellow raincoat leaning against his pew. Now I have him. Now I definitely have him. Et cum spiritu tuo, I yell out as loudly as possible. Then smile at those around me.

Soon, I've left the High Mass far behind and am following instead the progress of what must be the season's first fly. It's on the back of the young lady in front of me. It's crawling drowsily and without ceremony over her white dress. Her white chiffon dress with the frilly collar. The audacity of the creature amazes me. It's crawling towards her uncovered neck. What's it doing in the church anyway? They're not allowing flies into heaven now, are they? Pius Catholic flies? Repentant flies? Flies with table manners? Furious flies? Electric flies? Tragic flies? It'll lay its eggs on her neck and in her hair. They'll hatch by the thousands. She won't have a clue what's happening until it's too late. Maggots will hook themselves on to her flesh, will burrow into her brain and feast on it. She'll feel shame. Guilt. An urge for revenge. All because of that fly. The little man in the vestments—he couldn't handle an automatic, no way—is sprinkling incense on us. But that won't help. No tests have ever shown incense to be effective in killing flies. In fact, maggots have been known to breed particularly well beneath sanctuary floor-boards, in the beds of the overly celibate, be they priests, nuns or simply scared ordinary people.

I must save her. I must. I swat at the fly, my hand brushing her neck. She stiffens. People to either side glance at me in irritation, not bothering to turn their heads. They don't know the danger that flies represent. Or perhaps they choose to ignore it. Let someone else do the dirty work—that seems to be the motto these days. No one wants to take responsibility. Everyone cries victim and let the devil take the hindmost. The priest talks to the chorus, shaking his fist. The fly tries again, this time crawling down her back and not up, lifting its sticky dirty legs one at a time, stopping occasionally to rub the foremost feelers together like a miser admiring the pile of lucre before him.

I can see the long lacy goo, the footprints it leaves behind. I can really see them. My hand trembles in front of me. The chorus answers back brusquely and full of subdued meaning. I try to hold one hand with the other. Try to hold it back from its mission. Look at the Vendor. Concentrate on him. Ignore the fly. Forget about that fly. At the Vendor is where you should look. Focus! He's part of the choir answering briskly and to the subliminal point. I swat at the fly. My fingers thud against the girl's backbone. She stiffens again—and turns this time, her fresh young face reddening with anger.

I smile and whisper. Fly, I whisper, pointing at a dark spot on the chandelier that I take to be the culprit.

Do you mind! she hisses. Do you bloody mind! This is a place of worship. A holy place. Not a playground for immature buffoons.

A fly. A ...

She turns violently away again without allowing me to explain. I only hope she's in the habit of taking showers after attending Mass. That might save her from her maggot-y fate. The people around me stir and creak and shake their heads in my direction. The fly descends from the chandelier—

28

disappointed, I imagine, that it didn't have quite enough extra weight to bring that monstrous lighting apparatus ▪own—an▪ lan▪s on someone several rows away, too far for me to reach. I consider setting up a 'Pass-The-Word-Beware-Of-Fly' system whereby everyone in the church could be warned. Or perhaps have the priest slip it into his sermon: *Of Flies and the Ruination of Sartorial Elegance.* But decide against it. After all, the Lord helps those who help themselves. And these people ... these people are beyond saving. It's Ha▪es for the lot of them. A tantalizing prospect for the final act.

Worse yet, one can imagine my helplessness when the News Vendor turns out once more not to be the News Vendor. All this time I've been staring at the wrong person. An▪ now I've lost him. It's that fly's fault. That ▪amne▪ fly. Belongs in one of my partner's potions. I rush out of my seat an▪ bang square on into someone returning from Communion. He bites hard into the Host and then opens his mouth, realizing too late what he's done.

I continue out, as apologies are impossible in these holy matters. Be it accidental or out of ignorance. I wait in front of the church, this being the only exit save for several fire escapes on which I can't see a one-legge▪ man descending. Four yellow coats emerge, seventeen bald heads, three limps and several yellow birds pinned to the hats of twin sisters. But fortunately only one wooden leg. And I'm able to resume my vigil, the Lord be praised.

—

This night, I vividly remember tossing my youngest child (I think) into the air. He is so light, so weightless, he comes floating down like a balloon only slightly heavier than its surroundings. And happy. They are both happy. Even my adolescent daughter. I've never seen them so happy. He keeps calling me "Daddy" which makes me cry; his sister sits on the floor near the sofa, her head on my lap, her large eyes looking up at me. For once ignoring the iPad pounding out what passes for music on something called Spotify. I lean back and think about the church and why the News Vendor should want to go to Mass when he had his newspapers to satisfy him. Loss of faith, perhaps? At any rate, I don't like it.

When my partner comes home, I don't make my usual swift exit. Instead, we sit down to a family dinner. Well, it's actually quick-defrost frozen and grapefruit juice to wash it down but the candelabra makes up for it. After the children have been tucked into bed, my partner and I spend the rest of the evening memorizing terms of magic: *afreet, stolcheomancy, notarikon, cerne.* I reflect on the priest and the chorus and the fly and the people in the pit, especially the one in the white chiffon dress who didn't know she had footprints all over her back and maggots digging their way furiously towards her brain, looking for a place of warmth and moisture on which to breed. Perhaps she would never know (about those footprints, I mean) as most humans seem to have a funny sense of vision. And the ability to adapt to just about anything, even parasites straddling their neural connections. Perhaps that's the only connection.

—

General Notes of A Miscellaneous Nature: March 20th

He's taller than I first imagined, half an inch or so taller than me. And thinner. Nor is his breath what I thought it would be, considering I've never seen him brushing his teeth or conducting any sort of oral or dental hygiene. But rather than decay and putrefaction, it smells of fresh, as-yet-to-dry ink. Which makes sense after the fact. He holds out the magazine I've requested (an esoteric one on purpose so he has to root around for it) with both hands, like a chalice, like an offering. I dig into my pocket for the right change and drop it gently on the counter. The wooden leg slips a little as I nudge it with my foot. That allows me to notice that it's loose, unprotected, fair game.

Nice day, isn't it? I say. Even with the rain.

Nice day, he repeats. Even with the rain.

Face to face. His voice is smooth, not at all harsh or cracked as I imagine it should be after years of hawking papers. We're face to face and I'm looking into his stand. It too smells of yet-to-dry ink. It all does. As if unfinished. And damp paper. There's another door behind him. Not a back door. No. But obviously leading to another compartment, an inner chamber as it were. There is a lock on the door. He moves to another customer, leaving me to ponder the reason for the other door. He's about to return to me when I walk away, holding the magazine before my face and reading the first thing I find: the comics. Always the comics. Only these are in a language I barely understand—and certainly not well enough to get the jokes.

I'm struggling with the cartoons—a thin man dressed like a mouse trying to mount an elephant wife—when someone rips the magazine out of my hands and slaps me. Cuts my lip against a chipped tooth in desperate need of capping. I suck on the blood, watching the magazine come apart on the street, watching it float away on the wind. Some pieces jam behind the newsstand; others fall at the feet of The Hungry Artist. The Vendor is shaking his head, embarrassed at having to witness this, at having to see one of his products being treated so shabbily.

I look at him and shrug, as if to say it's not my fault, it's just a little misunderstanding. And she's crying, gritting her teeth and crying, pulling at the frayed sleeves of her blouse. She's not wearing a bra. She never wears a bra as the muscles must stay strong. Her nipples harden beneath the cool fabric. I tell her the nipples are finally hardening because there must be a cold wind blowing.

She's spitting at me, tiny globules of spit that in the end dwindle to nothing as they mix with the rain. She looks funny spitting nothing. I tell her she looks funny spitting nothing. I turn to ask the News Vendor: Doesn't she look funny? But he ignores me, busy pretending to read—from his private stock, no doubt. She's now yelling at me instead of spitting, yelling all kinds of words that rot what has been till now a pleasant day. She shouts stuff like I've made the children ashamed to be born and feeling guilty for growing up and that they never smile any more. I turn away as she falls down on the street, imploring me to come home before it's too late. I turn away, as she rises again and hurls threats at me and promises to take revenge, to make my life a living hell, to turn my children against me. I turn away, blushing to have the Vendor see me this way, and slink off into the nearest alley.

—

That is the night of the so-called attempted assault. But I don't mean it. I just want to see if I could harden the girl's nipples. I tell her that; I promise that's all I wanted. But she laughs and hikes up her skirt so easily, with such experience, and pulls down her panties so quickly that she gives me no chance to explain. I stumble away with her laughing on the ground, daring me to come and get some more if I have the guts.

I go home instead and make up to my partner by placing my head between her solid breasts and promising not to leave her again. I even promise to get myself a job so she can stay home with the children. She doesn't want to stay home with the children. She wants to continue working so we can buy a house of our own, a house in the mountains where the air is blue and the Big Dipper pours strands of gold into our eyes. Fine, fine, I say. We'll both work, then. And hire a nanny. After all, I do have several years of college under my belt and that should be enough for me to find a half-decent job somewhere. As a clerk maybe. As an insurance clerk maybe. Or a bank teller. Or a real estate agent. I have always been good at selling.

She claps her hands and cries for joy. I've never seen her happier or more excited. Or more anxious to make love. It is the least I can do so I lie on the side of the bed fingering her with one hand and holding a pair of black panties in the other. She moans with delight and I feel good, like a Good Samaritan should. In the end, however, all it does is add to the strain of my final departure ten days hence.

III.

The task I have set myself proves simpler than I had at first envisioned. Much simpler and at the same time more delicate and time consuming. All goes according to the meticulous plan I have sketched out in my mind. The main difficulty turns out to be one I hadn't thought of (as a difficulty, I mean) until it is too late to do anything about it. And that is how to allay the natural suspicions of my partner (and who could blame her for thinking I had found someone else?), how to fade out of her life and into my own, how to leave my beautiful children—such beautiful children—without hurting them beyond repair.

These questions are especially plaguing during my last few days at home, near the end of March, when all I can do is sit on the sofa and drum my fingers—too nervous even to type. In the long run, I have no choice but to simply and unceremoniously fling them to the wind with the devil-may-care attitude of "sauve qui se peut."

Although it's silly and useless of me now to say I knew it would, it all does turn out for the best. For my partner, for the children, for myself. Even for the News Vendor. I'm comfortably set in my new life. "Ensconced" I believe is the right word. I glimpse my partner often in the mornings trotting through the street with one child in her arms and the other clutched to her hand. They're on their way to school. She never smiles in her grim rush to catch the last bus. But what I have done can in no way be blamed for that. She has the same habit—of not smiling—even before I leave her (except that she'd regularly burst into spontaneous guffaws in the middle of the night after having babbled for several minutes during which she inevitably repeated a string of curses from her ever-present *Dictionary of Magic*).

Not that everything is hunky-dory. There are moments of insanity even now, though I'd like to believe they've all been left behind in those three rooms. Moments when I wish to pass my hand along the curve of her pelvic bone or to stroke the head of a child as they're bundled by me. But I also know that, if I ever succumbed to these urges, I would be forever re-attached, my hand trapped between her legs like an extra appendage, and only an axe would be able to separate us—with God knows what damage.

I'm grateful this urge vanishes when she vanishes. For she always manages to catch that last bus. Always. Even when it has already closed its doors and moved away from the curb. At these times, it comes to an abrupt halt, the driver yawning and knowing that, no matter what he does with the gas pedal, the bus will wait for her patiently, like a well-trained dog. The only explanation I can think of is the children.

I'm therefore amazed each time she mounts a bus that she doesn't simply discard them after their usefulness is past. I'd be prepared to pick them up as they came rolling down the sidewalk towards me. To spirit them away to some hiding place—sewer, bird's nest, whatever—where I could raise them and teach them things no one else knows. This is, I realize, just another form of the same insanity. When the time came to act, I'd let them roll by me to be deposited into a gutter. Then, I'd hold the bus by its back fender till they were safely on it again, none the worse for wear.

I've no idea what measures she took (or is taking) to find me. Most likely none. Most likely, she's expecting me home momentarily, will continue to expect me for years to come—stirring dinner with one hand, holding a recipe book for witches' brews in the other, gently pushing the youngest away with her foot when he comes too near the hot stove.

As yet, there's been no mention of my name in the papers (unlike the News Vendor, I read them all avidly), no Personal ad for a "John Doe-Sweetie Pie-Honeybunch" missing from his apartment since the morning of April First (no joke). Please return if found intact. Please return even if slightly damaged. Please return even if irreparable and must be glued together. Reward for him in love and/or kisses; for you, a finder's fee to be negotiated. All transportation and other charges will be paid by me. His eternally loving and forgiving partner. P.S.: The sad truth is that the children (he has two, one four, one nine) ask for their dear dear papa each night before they go to bed. And they cry. Oh how they cry. They're used to hearing his fantastic tales (of sailing ships and sealing wax) as they fall asleep. His when-we-two-became-one picture—he knows which one I mean—is kept upside-down on the dresser, ready to be dusted and polished upon his return to the household.

Moral censure for my actions may be appropriate but not welcomed. Nor is sympathy for that matter. There are facts, numerous and even contradictory facts, which you do not as yet have in your possession, which you might never obtain and at which you are presently only guessing for the sole purpose of passing judgement. Her incantations, vilifications and curses? Only practice runs for the annual convention of the Association of Amateur Witches, of which she's a dues-paying member. There was and is nothing personal in them at all, nothing to do with me. In fact, the reverse is true.

Her laughter is the same—a series of regulated and well-modulated cackles just meant to keep the copper cauldron bubbling. You're perhaps tallying the reasons I might have for leaving her: my jealousy and embarrassment that she was required—as a condition of her employment—to dance topless for certain hours of the day, with said hours increasing by the week, to climb onto tables and spread her buttocks for close inspection; my anger at the perpetual offers she received from other men—offers she claimed to have always turned down (but could I be sure?); my disgust at the smell of cigarettes and whisky her body acquired through something akin to osmosis; my feelings of neglect at her excessive love for the children.

But these, as well as countless others I've forgotten or am not willing to reveal, had and have no influence on my decision. None whatsoever. How could they? It is the task that has pulled me away. Nothing but the task. If there's anything to be understood here, to be gleaned, let that be it. Otherwise ... otherwise, I'll be forced to retract everything, to say I have no strong-breasted partner or beautiful children. That would mean having to start all over again. At a mental hospital perhaps or the bottom of a wishing well. No, no. I have only mentioned them to show where my difficulties lay once everything had been decided—and how unexpected these difficulties have been.

—

Notes On Things To Be Done Before
Final Leave-Taking: March 23rd

1. *On March 24th, visit the museum—specifically the fine arts museum—for the first time. Get a car♦ for their noon tour. Revision: Get two car♦s.*
2. *Buy an axe (two-bladed optional). Keep it sharpened.*
3. *Check on the amount of cash in the cookie jar. About four hundred. How much should I take? How much do I deserve to take? None, as I've earned none of it. Then, I guess I'd better take it all.*
4. *See about a hotel room. Needed by April 1st. Must be above the News Vendor's and facing the same way as his room. Should be easy to get as there are always plenty of vacancies.*
5. *Use some of the money to get my partner a new beaver tail (hers is splitting) and enlarged dictionary of magic (even if she does only use online resources these days). Call it a going-away gift. A touch of symbolism.*
6. *Have some photos taken of me and the children to leave with them as a remembrance. I was, after all, their father. Even if only briefly. On secon♦ thought ...*

B: Consequent Action Following

Upon A Necessary Prelude

I

April 1st

It's time to begin. I feel liberated and for once the modernist/post-modernist/ultramodernist abstract paintings and sculptures in the museum don't depress me, give me a headache or confuse my sense of direction. In fact, they almost seem to make sense amid the more traditional, photo-like studies. Or those of plump naked women in quasi-erotic poses (but no match for my partner). And the almost-three dimensional holographic installation of a flat screen TV fighting a laptop with a chocolate-swirl cell phone as reluctant referee feels in some ways as the most real thing there.

Meanwhile, the woman who's both old and blind and spills sand talks on and on about paradoxes, contradictions and anti-logical reversals as she fingers the crevasses of whatever comes her way: nude virgins, husky male athletes and cherubic children alike—and deftly avoids the angular disturbances of the cubists and surrealists which can cut the unsuspecting.

"Cool thighs," she says, rubbing a philosopher's chunky arm. "Never been savaged by human hands. Marble produces such cool unrapable thighs. To make up for the Sabine Women, I guess. Do you know the story of Pygmalion? (I nod. Of course, I do.) Of course, you do. One could stroke these thighs for centuries and they'd remain as cool, as distant, as far-fetched … Pygmalion. Yes, Pygmalion. 'Detesting the faults beyond measure which nature has given to women,' he produced a creature unsullied by womb and without umbilical cord. There aren't any Pygmalions left, are there? (I nod again, just at the moment I realize she can't see me. And yet, why is it I get the impression she pauses and waits for my nod—or a wink perhaps?) No more Pygmalions; no more Galateas."

She talks while I stand near her, waiting. Unsure what to do. The guards forgive her intimate fingerings the moment they realize she's blind. They come bustling up to her from their posts beside the statues, the set speech already forming, their tongues already in position for the lecture: "Hey, ma'am, can't you read? That's not ..." And then she turns towards them ever so slowly, whipping out a snake-like smile and holding out her hands, eyes blank and lacking pupils. The speech gets caught in their throats, comes out as a series of hisses and sputters. They mumble apologies and hasten away, afraid to look back. Or if they do return, it's with broom in hand to sweep up the sand.

This makes her all the bolder. She begins to rub her entire body against the statues, to stroke them unreservedly in what would be their most private parts—if they weren't so exposed in the first place. At one point, I have to restrain her from pulling up her rag of a skirt and trying to mount the fist of one of the fleshier specimens. Now, after my warning that the gods don't take too kindly to humans who muscle in on their territory, she confines herself to testing which have the largest breasts and hips, bellies and buttocks, pubes and penises, which are period pieces and which for all ages.

After a while, you get the impression they're softening under her deft hands, that she can actually squeeze them, can actually make dents in them and cause them to sigh contentedly. But they revert immediately to marble at my touch. She bends over and ever so softly ever so gently kisses a nipple. Or the crook of an arm. Then she too sighs contentedly. In the future, she'll be here every chance she gets, groping and grappling, till finally the guards tire of her and have her carted away—stiff and unbending, a woman well on the road to becoming a statue herself. And all the better for it.

—

I found her sitting against the sharp corner of the windowless building, prophesying to the dirt, wrappers, garbage bags and rags in front of her, half-buried in sand: "And there will come a day ... a day ... yes there will ... a fast approaching day ... when the blind will see and the sighted will be blind. Yes. And the loss of limbs will be a natural occurrence like unto the species of star-fish and other jellies, reptiles and arachnids. This new person is born daily, born of my pure spit and the dumb earth's fertility." She spat. A noise in her throat like someone sawing wood. She spat again and I spoke up, solemnly: "And there will come a day when paper will become light and light will scour the earth clean. When the dimensions will flatten into two. I'm the prophecy come true. Greetings to the prophet. Or should I say prophetess?"

The spit stopped in mid-air, dribbled in globs down the front of her face, into her wispily thin white beard and across the ropes of her neck. Something, I learned later, was always dribbling down the front of her face into this quasi-beard. Shaking and trembling, she groped towards me, pushing her feet through the sand, through the pile of still-smouldering rubbish. Shaking and trembling, she passed her hands (that felt like dried bark) slowly over my face, checking each depression and protuberance as if I were a lamb or a calf. Or a piece of valuable heirloom furniture. Shaking and trembling, she embraced me and hailed me as the new human, with tears from unsighted eyes, the new human born of holy spit and the goddess's mud, risen to lead her beyond this land of maculate desolation over the bridge of restful freedom to … to … to … Her voice petered away and she was left muttering to herself, holding on to my arm with enough pressure to momentarily interrupt the flow of blood.

("I found her sitting"—this wasn't strictly true, if it implies I was taken by surprise. Yes, she was sitting in front of the building on that particular day but I'd heard her speaking in this way a number of times before—on the tiny urban park bench as I wrote parts of my "Notes", at the side of the windowless building with an ear against an earthquake-caused crack, in the park walking to and fro and creating her own trail between a pair of shrivelled, stunted cypresses. In other words, I could easily predict where she would be and what she would say on the day she was needed—and I was in perfect position both to respond and to act.)

As I spoon-fed her the chicken soup, she talked incessantly, spitting particles of it back into my face. Noodles caught in her beard (naturally) and were strained of their broth. Several would fall out later at the museum. She talked mostly of her prophecies, how no one paid attention to her, her valuable years in a mental hospital to round out her education, the visions she was privileged to entertain behind her dead eyes, the short-circuiting of her neural synapses, and her direct connection to the original mother goddess in her cave, the one who used to stuff children back into her womb.

Imagine, she said, they had thought she was crazy. (I was beginning to entertain a similar opinion.) Crazy! When in fact she was educating them. Were all the old blind prophets treated that way? Only when they had news no one wanted to hear, I answered. She said it was just selfishness on the part of the people. Fear of being brushed aside by a newer, stronger, more effective breed. "Made not of flesh but of light. The everlasting image. The bearer of the torch of enlightenment."

I led her through the city, shuffling noisily a few feet behind me, her hand on my shoulder for guidance. Past the News Vendor who, I could see, approved of what I was doing. Past the neon-flashing club where snap-shots in the window told of the delights waiting inside and a tieless drunk still relentlessly blew warm air at my partner's nipples, just to the right of a mole that kept growing with a volcanic fury. Over the bridge that connected the two ends of the city and held them together against the force of the brackish water below, against the tidal surge that was constantly cleaving and slicing and lapping up earth.

And at last into the museum, a momentous stone monster built to outlast the ages, the place in which to store all the temporary, in-the-moment fads before they are replaced by others. This included close to the entrance a presently empty area with a banner in fancy type reading: "The Gutenberg Era: 1439-202X" and below it: "Made possible by a generous donation from the Schloss Corporation."

Hmm, a pretty good run for a fad. Anyway, no time to tarry or reflect on what might eventually fill the space. I checked my pocket for the cards and the self-lock plastic bag that writhed on its own. It was time to begin.

—

A noodle slithers from her beard and is squashed beneath her feet— one more pattern in the vein-streaked marble floor. I hold out the cards which allow us to join the Golden Ager tour of the museum's medieval weaponry collection. This is hidden away in the basement among the pillars and dampness of another building—the remnant foundations of the previous structure. A necessary palimpsest. Here, they have catapults and cross-bows, shields, swords, battle-axes, maces, clubs, lances, hauberks and other pieces of Vulcan-pounded armour. I have taken the time to read up on them, to learn thoroughly their uses. Another section contains a complete set of torture instruments: whips for atonement and flogging; a metal container much like a barbecue pit for burning the soles of heretics' feet; racks and manacles of all kinds; a cage to be placed over the recalcitrant one's face.

She passes her fingers over them all, commenting on their structure and purpose and their efficacy. She's just hitting her stride when the tour guide suddenly decides to call it quits, spurred on no doubt by an unforeseen influx of ants, spiders and millipedes, many of which have slipped out of a suddenly-dropped plastic bag and are now very busily crawling in phalanxes up the legs of the slower matrons. Some are beginning to itch, to scratch in places where they shouldn't in public.

I giggle. She asks what could be so funny in a place that records man's inhumanity to man. And woman, I remind her. Remember the witches. Ah, yes. They had it easy, she says. They were just raped, had their children yanked with pliers from their bellies and burned at the stake.

We follow the fleeing tour till I'm able to duck behind a pillar and pull her along with me. She doesn't struggle. Nor does she need any explanation or instructions as to what I'm doing. We're not missed, a body count not being deemed necessary when coming *out* of a torture chamber. The door is locked and bolted above us. Only the authentic rag-and-tar torches smoke away against the walls, leaving their dark, sooty halos above them, a reverse aura. And there's the faint whirring of air-conditioning units sucking the smoke away, making sure the temperature and humidity are just so. Wouldn't want the instruments of destruction to warp and thus fail to do their assigned tasks.

I am certain the guards pacing overhead can't hear us. I know this from my previous visit to the museum when I'd allowed myself to be locked in. At that time, I had screamed till my voice was hoarse; I had run back and forth at full speed; I had pounded on the walls and ceiling. Nothing. No one heard me. Or else, if they had, they paid no attention. Just the remnants of a poor, tortured spirit, ghosts of anguish past. Best to leave such creatures to their own suffering. To let them slowly fade away like some piece of suddenly useless technology. Ah, I remember the antique printing press in another part of the museum, with its wooden blocks. That, too, might make a fine torture machine. An inundation of pure propaganda. And one mustn't forget its latest incarnation: the pixillated screen.

My blind friend runs into a spider's web and immediately starts a new harangue on the creatures soon to be developed (the spider is trying desperately to escape from her beard), the creatures with their ability to rejuvenate limbs and perhaps autophagous as well. Which in her opinion (the spider has dropped to the floor, floating on a strand that still dangles from her beard) would greatly enhance their chances of staying alive in a world of dire straits and barren crags where they could, as a last resort, eat parts of themselves. The ultimate re-cycling program. She dwells in great detail on someone chewing his own leg stump or arm-pit: how to cook it, salt it, perhaps store it until needed.

My stomach threatens to heave. I inspect the weapons and try to ignore what she's saying. At moments like these, I wish she were dumb as well as blind so that I could have a little silence to prepare myself properly. But you can't have everything and there's no way of doing it on my own. I found that out the last time I was here. So all I can do is sit down against a post, shut my eyes and listen to her constant chatter, praying all the while for closing time to come soon—as I wouldn't want to be interrupted by an unscheduled, spur-of-the-moment tour or some pale-faced ninny of a scholar doing original research on King Arthur's undescended left testicle.

When I open my eyes again, she's still talking, but I realize I must've slept for it's now past closing time. I touch her arm and tell her I'm ready. She nods and smiles. I lead her to the nearest rack, the most sophisticated one, and let her feel the points of contact, the shackles, the ropes, the wheel that gathers everything together and stretches bones into funny (as in warped) shapes. Then, I lie down on it—a little nervous, perhaps, but not overly concerned—and she fumbles about till she has strapped me in.

I'm not at all worried that she'll forget me and simply keep turning the wheel with reckless abandon till I'm in several bloody pieces or have become a huge elongated rubbery monster. The latest mutant. Cousin to *The Fantastic Four*. No, that doesn't worry me. She needs me and won't do anything to really hurt me. I am, after all, one of the new creatures—born of her spit and the goddess's mud, who'll lead her over the ... over the ...

She has to strap me in a second time as, on turning the wheel to tighten the bonds, my left hand slips loose. It's hard to make her understand the problem. My instructions to her were not to listen to my screams or any pleadings to be released. These are only natural, remnants of an understandable urge to self-preservation. She agrees. So, when I begin to shout that one of my arms isn't strapped in properly, she thinks I only want the pressure slackened for a moment—and this could be fatal to the overall project. "Clever. Very clever." The problem of having a blind accomplice act as torturer. "Too clever to fool me. I'm a simple woman."

I shout again, calling her a few choice names. Finally, her sensitive touch discerns that the thong is truly loose on one side and not tightening properly. "Not so clever after all." I crane my neck to watch her feeling along my arm to the wrist where she searches about re-attaching the padded thong. "I knew it was too clever to be true. I just knew it." The last of the noodles falls on my face; an ant crawls up my leg. I try to shake it off, but it hangs on, tickling me fiendishly. I strain against the thongs, trying to get at it. I pray for the pain to start. And then I pray for it to stop.

No one can feel pain until he's feeling it. Perhaps not even then to the fullest extent, to the bone-raw bottom. The sum total of my philosophy on pain. I've tried to imagine for many days—since the conception of my plan—just what it would be like stretched out on the rack, just what kind of pain it would come down to after all the others had been surpassed. Impossible. The other pains are not surpassed. Never. They're simply added on to the next one ... and the next one ... and the next one. The pain breaks up into infinite pieces connected only through neurons and nerve-endings.

I keep screaming "Enough! Let me go! I've had enough!" until I faint. My eyes seem to stand out on stalks like those of some alien creature no longer able to breathe properly in Earth's fetid air. "Enough! I can't take any more! Please. That's enough!" The sweat pops up out of the pores and wells over in torrents down my face, burning my eyes. I've always fancied myself a fairly courageous man with a high pain threshold. At least metaphorically. If you don't believe me, witness the leaving of my partner and children. Now, I know that only metaphorically can I make that claim. She scoffs at me, leans over and, after feeling for the ridges of my forehead, my cheek-bones, laughs in my face.

"It's all right," she repeats continuously in a slightly mocking tone. "It's all right ... it's all right to surrender quickly and without putting up a fight when someone is torturing you for secrets or their pleasure ... for deep secrets or their false-bottomed pleasure ... it's all right because ... because you know ... because the torture won't cease until ... until ... until you tell them all you know and maybe it won't stop even then ... not even then ... till death do you part ... but self-inflicted pain, self-inflicted torture must always ... must always be carried through to the end ... the end ... the end ... Don't you agree?"

I faint. On awaking from a dream in which I'm on a hot desert island being tortured on a rack, I confess all my secrets to someone who insists that the name I've given him is not the one written down, to someone I keep referring to as the Commandant. She doesn't want to hear, covers her ears, orders me to scream instead. I tell her all there is to know about my sex life. ("My partner is an incorrigible screwer. She loves to get laid, any way and anytime I feel like it. Cats and dogs get my attention once in a while but not too too often. They're hard to catch and even harder to hold down.")

I beg her to listen to me. To my sex life. It's important. I tell her about the girl I raped in the alley. She listens, a grim, disapproving expression on her face. It's obvious the new human need not resort to that sort of thing. No, she raped *me*, I bellow. She did! She did! Can't you understand that? I just said I raped her to cause a stir, to get your attention. Look, pull my trousers down. Look, I'm still wearing the black panties she gave me as a souvenir. Feel. She slips his hand into my trousers and feels the silky smooth panties. Ugh, she says. How disgusting. You should never admit to something you haven't done. Better to have done it.

See, I told you. And my kids aren't even mine. No. That's right. They aren't. Not really. Not at all. They belong to the bus driver by default. They do! Yes, my partner straddles the gear-shift and becomes pregnant by it. Yes, every day. Oh my, oh my, oh my. That's why the bus waits for them, for its children. Does that qualify them as genuinely new creatures or simply untenable hybrids? Destined for evolution's junk heap, the genetic scrapyard, the spare parts depot?

I faint. On awaking from a dream in which I have spilled semen all over myself after being tortured to death, I tell her my partner is a witch, a white witch, a wonderful white witch whom I love very much and can't live without. But I have a task to accomplish and she'd only get in the way, even if she only got out of the way. Do you understand now? I explain the circumstances of my leaving. ("It was the sunrise that finally did it. I sat up in bed with her still sleeping beside me, her breasts rising softly beneath the sheets, and the sunrise of this particular morning was exactly like the sunrise of all the other particular mornings. And the song on the radio was, the same as always, *Come Sail Away*. So I finished dressing and left. Left her sleeping with her breasts rising softly beneath the sheets.")

She agrees—but I realize it's only out of politeness—that I had no choice. I'm glad she agrees even if only out of politeness but I know she would have preferred something more drastic, more elemental. A multiple murder-suicide perhaps. My partner and kids left in a pool of their own blood, gutted, experimented upon and then stitched back together. To themselves rise as new creatures, as polite Dr. Frankenstein monsters, stomping full speed ahead in the world's vast uncertainty, brains replaced by AI machinery, all the human tragedy squeezed out.

I faint. On awaking from a dream in which the News Vendor with two good legs suddenly (re-growth? reverse autophagy? simple micro-surgery decades down the road?) is offering me the soiled and fly-spotted Host at Communion, a Host which I chew sacrilegiously like gum, I find that I'm free. But still unable to move. My spinal column feels as if it has been disconnected. My legs dangle uselessly. The skin on my body sags. I hear bones, vertebrae, tendons, cartilage trying to snap back into place. The walls of my stomach attempt a desperate touching, sloshing through hydrochloric acid to kiss.

I turn my head slowly. She's asleep on the floor, back against a pillar, snoring heavily and moving in jerks from one position to another. A lady bug, a flash of orange in an otherwise drab-grey world, flitters above her head. It becomes entangled in her hair and then bursts out again. There are millipedes milling about the floor, centipedes sensing the air. Slipping and sliding through the sand as if they're having fun. I have to move with care, lifting myself up gently. A sudden twist and I'm back on the rack, caught in the same painful vortex. I nudge her with my foot. She jumps immediately awake.

At precisely noon, the tour will again be hurried through on its way to more interesting exhibits. Someone will slow it up by stopping to examine the rack and commenting on the wet spot near its centre. Those dirty rats, someone else will shout to general laughter. The bugs left over from the previous day will get to work on the matrons.

We'll wait behind a pillar and join in at exactly the same point we left off yesterday. Nothing will have changed. Except that every few steps I'll have to lean on her shoulder for support. She'll console me and tell me I've performed splendidly for a novice. That will make me proud and my head will swell greatly. Somewhere inside it, perhaps on an unused portion of my brain, will be a balloon. I'll make no attempt to think out its colour.

She'll pass her hands one more time across the thighs of the virgins, the athletes, the angelic children, kiss their softening pectorals with even softer lips. Till I return, she'll say. Keep the faith, babies. Hasta la vista. I'll constantly feel like vomiting, an urge impossible to keep down. Once outside, we'll head for the bridge. She'll be talking again, will be beginning another monologue or picking up an old one exactly where she'd left it off to tend to me. I'll tell her, to no avail, to shut up. Shut up! Shut up! Shut up!

Right at the centre of the bridge, above the ragtag navy of small unpainted boats and rusted tugs that rise and fall one at a time yet with the sweet cadence of the water, above the sheds and warehouses that no amount of repairing will bring back to an original lustre, above the shiny railroad tracks and the rusted spur lines almost completely hidden by growths of cat-tails and adder's-tongue ferns, above all this, I'll vomit. I'll vomit and watch the flecks of red and green and yellow spiral at different speeds at different densities like foul confetti down into the graciously accepting water. I'll vomit till I can feel portions of my stomach about to come up as well, eaten away by the acid of pain and fear.

She'll pat me on the back again and laugh and say that's good, that's very good, you're finally being purged. Of what? Of clinging humanity. Of the residue of human kindness. Of culture's tendrils and civilization's claws. Seagulls will swoop down in long elegant lines—like contoured flying tubes—to gather everything up before it dissolves or sinks away forever.

—

I barely make it back to my room. She massages my muscles, kneads the thick cords that have formed along my shoulder blades and down my thighs up into my buttocks which are a sickly mottled blue colour. I sleep all the day in a tense ball, fearful of movement, of snapping a sinew or ligament with any quick jerk or spasm. When I awake later in the evening to the sound of praying (ugh!) in the room below mine, I immediately measure myself, using a yard stick and a mark against the wall. I find I've increased my height by a quarter of an inch. That is enough for me. That will have to do. I don't think I could go through that again. It will definitely have to do.

I lie back on the bed and look around the hotel room, a satisfied grin on my face. The sound of buzzing disturbs my reverie. A bee, its legs heavily laden with pollen, has slipped in through the slightly open window. It is bouncing from spot to spot along the wallpaper, the flower-pattern wallpaper. Does it know somehow that the wallpaper resembles a field of dandelions? It flies further into the room until it hits a corner. Then, it turns, looking for the way out. I point at the window and whisper directions as if in a play. Stage left, I whisper. Stage right.

Several times, it swings close to my face before whirling away again. It hangs there in front of me, wings whirring rapidly to keep it still. Finally, after thudding against the window pane and becoming entangled in the flowery curtains, it escapes into the street. I push my face against the window to follow its path. It is floating danger-ously close to the rush hour traffic when it finally disappears from my line of vision.

When I was younger, such an event would have disconcerted me. I would have spent the rest of the evening wondering if the bee had made it back to its hive or had been flattened against a tractor-trailer windshield, golden powder splattered in fractal directions. Now, it is out of sight out of mind. We become inured to the fate of others, I say lugubriously. That is our fate.

II.

April 3rd

She informs me casually, while sitting on my bed and slurping up her second bowl of chicken noodle soup, that it would be better if we do the job in the dark. It makes little difference to her, of course, but she has serious doubts about my ability to lie still at the crucial moment. I agree and turn off the light. Only the occasional flash of the hotel's neon sign prevents absolute darkness. I remove my trousers (oh, squirming in those lovely and silky black panties again) and lie in the centre of the room, on the wide-planted and cool wooden floor away from obstructions and obstacles. I breathe in deeply. Then slowly let the air out.

"Hold yourself steady now," I hear her voice whispering in the dark. "That's it. Very steady. Don't move a muscle now."

Her hand searches for the right spot on my thigh, the proper point. She squeezes the flesh. I spread my legs wider and stare up at what must be the ceiling. I pray that it's over before my eyes get accustomed to the dark and I can see what she's doing. The perspiration gathers in rivulets on my face and chest, flows down the sides of my legs, sticking them to the floor. I reach up to pass my hands through a shock of curly hair. Find instead only moist, glossy skin with but a fringe of hair.

—

It was while I slept that she cropped my hair and then shaved my head with a straight razor. There were two small cuts on my forehead. Either her blindness had let me down or I'd moved without warning. They ran parallel with each other like wrinkles or railroad tracks. I stood before the mirror in awe, staring at this suddenly old, suddenly decrepit creature. My head was bumpy and uneven. Already, blue stubble had started to sprout through my skull. I'd have to shave it every second or third day if I wanted to keep it presentable.

"You struggled in your sleep," she said the following day as we prepared for lunch. "That cost you those cuts. You may as well know it now and not take it out on me. I know what you were thinking when you saw them. A little revenge, maybe? Now the only person you can take it out on is yourself, right? I couldn't understand why you would resist. You have a beautiful skull. Few people are blessed with skulls like that. I can still feel it beneath my hands—a wonderful, illustrious skull. Well-formed and full of character. A phrenologist's delight. Pity it had to be covered this long with hair."

I pulled the cap further down on my head, trying to keep from catching a chill. She slurped up her noodles.

"It's better if we do it in the dark. Don't you think? Otherwise, I'm afraid you won't be able to lie still when the time comes. And that'll be a pity. A real pity."

—

The hotel's neon light flashes and she's silhouetted against the wall, like one of those giant shadows from a cave fire. On the upswing. On the point of equilibrium. On the downswing. I roll out of the way at the last moment. The axe imbeds itself into the floor beside me, rattling the room. In the dark again, I can hear her heaving and straining as she tries to dislodge it. Ironically, it's my hands and not my legs that shake. A loose nail prods my back. I panic and jump up.

"Stay away," I shout. "Leave me alone! What kind of maniac are you anyway?"

"Your kind," she says, straining and heaving. "The kind you need. Only a maniac would take this job in the first place."

She finally succeeds in pulling out the axe but falls backwards to the floor with the effort. I stumble about looking for the door, for a way out. Only to scrape my shins against the edge of the bed. I swear—and give myself away. Methodically, she combs the room. Moves easily among the few pieces of furniture. Stops to listen for my movements or perhaps even the sound of my breath.

"Your heart beats too swiftly," she says with alarming calmness. "Pit-a-pat, pit-a-pat. No matter how still you stand. Even if you hold your breath, I'll find you. Even then. Now stop this nonsense and submit. It's for your own good, for your good only. The theory has to be tested. Otherwise, it'll remain in the abstract, in that unsatisfying and godless realm. You understood that once and will come to understand it again when it's all over. But right at this moment …"

By the light of "Hotel Azazel" (with one of the "z's" missing) I can see her outline in the dark. She stands, axe across her chest like a warrior-priest, guarding the door. Or like a nun there to ensure no boys cross into the girls' side of the school. I'm crouched in a corner between the bed and the window, determined not to give her easy access to me.

"Ah, naughty boy. You're thinking perhaps of slipping out the window to the safety of the street, aren't you? I must warn you, there's no fire escape. Not even a ledge. The assistant manager was gracious enough to inform me. Ah, but you know that, too, don't you? With your mundane gift of sight. Nevertheless we do have a problem, you and I. If I come forward to ferret you out, you might slip behind me and make a dash for so-called freedom. If you attempt that dash for freedom, I shall be forced to hack at you, to most likely decapitate you. Or worse, maim you in unpleasant and quite accidental ways."

—

In the end, it was no glorious achievement to effect my escape. She waited patiently for several hours with the hope I would come to my senses. But I continued to act like a frightened animal. As if enlightened human nature had not yet reached me. She called me a bevy of obnoxious names—all justly deserved, mind you, threatened at one point to chop me into little pieces and then threw down the axe. Just like that.

I breathed a sigh of relief as she opened the door and groped her way out muttering to herself, head held erect with an air of moral superiority. The sight of her leaving, abandoning me, shocked me back to reality. I called after her and waved the axe in the air to indicate I was now ready. But she didn't hesitate for a moment and quickly disappeared down the stairs. I dared not shout too much or go after her for fear of running into the assistant manager who was already eying me in a most unfriendly way, in a way that indicated he was onto me.

—

The butcher shop ("Argos' Prime Meat—Wholesale & Retail") just down the street from the Absinthe A-Go-Go is white-tiled and spotless, with a shiny green and white awning and a sign on the door that reads: "These premises are protected against unwanted pests by a double system of doors that makes it impossible for both to be opened at the same time. Should one get in the front door, an odourless time-released pesticide harmless to all but insects will make sure it never gets to the second. Nor will any of our customers be bothered by the sight of creatures writhing in their death agony. We keep an employee on the premises for just that purpose."

Fortunately I come prepared by bringing my own—a beautifully patterned cockroach (call him "G") whose wings are like rainbows. (Okay, so I painted the original drab brown specimen. It has to make its presence felt, to let the world know it means business.) I hold it inside a glass box in my trouser pocket, enjoying the sensation of its frantic whirring and beating of wings.

There's only one customer in the place, a young woman in a blue chiffon dress with a frilly collar. She looks familiar but I can't quite place her. In any case, she's busy inspecting a gorgeous piece of Grade AAA meat being held out before her like an offering by the butcher's assistant. The butcher himself is slicing mortadella while his other helper sprinkles sawdust on the floor and occasionally rushes out to pick up dead insects between the two doors. I get the silly feeling they'll all break out in a tap dance at any moment. Maybe not so silly as they all have the right uniforms for it, including straw hats and green-and-white striped outfits. A pantomime. A vaudeville entertainment. Laurence Olivier. Vladimir and Estragon. Oh, to be so lucky.

When no one is looking, I pretend to inspect an imprisoned lobster claw sticking out of the tank and then release the cockroach. It makes a desperate flutter into the air, whirring and bouncing off the light. The effect is like announcing that a new strain of small-pox virus has been unleashed. Or that all cattle have been certified BSE positive. The butcher lets out a little cry, a gasp-like whimper, a moan-like moan, and covers his mouth while staggering back against the green-and-white tiled wall, forgetting all about the mortadella and the machine slicing it. The butcher's first assistant drops the proffered piece of meat on the counter and is joined by the butcher in chasing the cockroach. In their haste, they bump into one another, stumble, try to fit into the same space. The second assistant is frozen on the spot, simply rocking on the spot.

I whistle lightly, getting into the spirit with a passable rendition of *Flight of The Bumblebee*. (I guess *La Cucaracha* would have been more appropriate but I couldn't bring it to mind at the time.) The customer—I recognize her at last as the maggot-y young woman from the church—sweeps the air with her purse and then stomps out in disgust, paying no heed to the figure in the bloody apron who assures her they'll soon have the situation under control. She's not very good at listening, I say. Has her own fixed ideas about how things should go. Besides, who is she to complain, a woman who carries out her own insect incubation program? And someone who betrays her own brother? Or is it the other way around?

Then I start to whistle more loudly, plotting the quickest route to the meat-cutting machine—a series of gleaming blades that vibrate invisibly in the still air after having finished hacking at the processed clump of meat. I wonder how easily it'll cut through cloth. Or should I lower my trousers to speed it along. The butcher manages to regain some semblance of dignity and opens the inner door to his shop. The first assistant tries to shoo the cockroach into the passageway. Instead, perhaps sensing the odourless pesticide, the non-smell of death, it loops in the air, does a reverse turn and insinuates itself into the piece of glowing red beef that has been dropped on the counter. The butcher, now on the verge of hysteria, orders his assistant back. He'll take care of this.

"The swatter," he whispers, holding out his hand like a surgeon about to perform a delicate operation. "Where's the …?"

And then he remembers they had thrown it out, conducted a farewell ceremony over it when the special doors were installed. He chooses instead the broadest blade in the shop, more machete than knife. Holding it on the flat edge and shutting his eyes to the horror, he squashes the cockroach against the meat. The second assistant chooses that moment to come out of his trance. The two assistants breathe a sigh of relief in unison, turn to one another, and shake hands. Then gather near the butcher. While the three of them lean over the tainted meat like mourners over a coffin, I leap across the counter and lift my leg against the cutter. But my foot catches in the cord and unplugs the machine. The knives whirl to a sudden stop.

"Hey!" the butcher shouts, surging towards me. "What… what are youse doing? What de hell do youse think …? What're youse, fuckin' nuts? Get de fuck outta here before I calls de police!"

I move back out of reach. The glass bottle falls out of my pocket, bounces across the sawdust floor.

"Lunatic!" the butcher screams, turning the colour of freshly-slaughtered beef. "You're de one who let de cockroach loose in here, ain't youse? I'm gonna kill youse." He waves the machete. "I'm gonna make mince meat outta youse."

The assistants manage to hold the butcher back momentarily as I dash past him. He shakes himself loose and rushes after me down the street, holding the spoiled beef in one hand and waving the machete-knife in the other. But he's overweight and has trouble breathing so he doesn't chase me more than a block before bending over. I turn and smile, letting him know there are no hard feelings on my part. But those are certainly tears in his eyes as he hugs the meat to his chest, as he brings it up to his lips for a last kiss.

I start to run again, not over the bridge but down into the streets below it, feeling the hot surge of my calves and thighs—armed, triggered and ready to explode. These streets are invariably dead-ends, leading to the arm of the bay that necessitated the bridge in the first place. Rooming houses, dilapidated and covered by rusty Coke signs, turn into even more dilapidated warehouses and sheds. I'm almost under the bridge now, almost at the spot where—if I could go back in time—I'd be showered with my own vomit.

A row of rotting boats wavers in the sludge. I wonder which one belongs to the News Vendor. Shiny rails lead to the fronts of loading docks and shipping yards where spurs, mostly unused, slide off into head-high grass. I kneel down and place my ear against a rail—a trick I learned from watching Saturday morning Westerns. *Caboose on the loose!* Ah good. There's a train predicted in the not-too-distant future.

—

The butcher-shop incident proved not only embarrassing but silly as well. There was no need for it save to point out the confused state of my thinking at the time. The meat-cutting machine wasn't even made for my purposes. It would have mangled instead of slicing cleanly. That's if the bone didn't stop it. Added to this, I'd never witnessed a more pitiable figure than the butcher (poor soul who had not done anyone—other than a few protein-rich animals—harm, who served the public to the best of his albeit limited ability) clutching that cockroach-spoiled meat.

However, I had been desperate. Events were conspiring to foil my plans. The News Vendor still sat contentedly in his stand, either selling or reading his goods. My partner swivelled her hips from rote and held up her nipples, sometimes blue from the constant rubbing against customers. The blind woman, having forgotten both me and my inexcusable cowardice, was once more at her familiar post in front of the windowless building, once more trying to entice some passer-by, more attuned to her words, to volunteer for her new humanity experiments. In exchange for a couple of garbage bags slowly being emptied of sand.

Good luck, I whispered. You have nature to contend with. Human nature. Your goddess (and the socialists) failed to take that into account.

—

I pull up the left leg of my trousers and place my thigh across the railroad track. Though it's late evening, the flesh is hot and sticky where it rests on the metal rail. I lie flat on my back and look up. I see the shadow of someone leaning over the bridge railing, scattering shredded pieces of paper into the water. Some of them float over me, wafted by the gentle breeze. Some incriminating documents, no doubt, put through the office shredder.

The seagulls are at it again, thinking there's more food, more manna falling from the sky. One of them has a streamer caught in its beak and tries frantically to free itself. Others chase the streamer and peck at it. Gravel is pushing through my shirt and imbedding itself into my skin. I shift positions slightly. The person on the bridge, emboldened, seems to be pouring the shredded paper out by the bucketful, blanking the entire sky above me. Must have lots of secrets to unload. Where's that train? That train, comes the echo. That train. Is it better on my back or on my stomach? I've always assumed it would be better on my back with a vision of the heavens before me. But now I can't find anything to support that. For there are no heavens—just a lot of confetti. Maybe to celebrate a marriage between heaven and hell.

That train. There's that train. There's that train swerving along the edge of the bay, careening to one side. It can't slip off now. Oh no. It can't pile up now like a carelessly dropped accordion. That won't do. It just won't do. I notice a fly-covered fish-head near me on the track. Fling a stone at it. Shoo. The flies rise into the air in a black cloud. But settle right back down again. Again. Egg-gain. That's what they're doing. A-laying. Ensuring a future. The train will frighten them away. I can certainly rely on the train to scatter them to the wind. Or shatter them to the wind. Best to keep quiet. Unless I want a mouthful of confetti, of shredded secrets, I'd best keep it shut. Lips pressed firmly together. Save the screams for later. You'll need them, Kemo Sabe.

The train adjusts, shifts to the other side, straightens out. It's dancing, dancing now as the diesel turns the last corner and heads down the straightaway. Again my hands twitch and shake. The ground trembles. The earth moves. The rails hum. The flies gossip. Gravel scars my back. Is that me? Will that train, that damned train, see me too soon and stop? Screech to a spark-flashing halt? It can't. It mustn't.

A large truck is unloading shredded paper, the hydraulic system tilting back tons of it over the bridge. Must be government secrets. Medical experiments. The seagulls are swamped and can't breathe. Beak-to-beak resuscitation is in order. A peck by the bushel. Insemination if necessary. Artificial intelligence. Military intelligence. A Lem-Dick hybrid. There's that train. Here's that train.

It'll do it ... it'll do it ... it *will* do it. It can't be me. The flesh will be torn right off the bone and the bone will be torn right off the ... and the butcher hugs his piece of rump roast, holds it between his legs. No. No. Beef. His piece of beef. Cake. Jerks into it with all his might. Shoots off a creamy load. Scattering bits of cockroach. Shiny painted wings glistening in the light.

Am I going to scream? Shut my eyes? Bounce off the track with fear? It's only a few hundred metres away. Feet, ankles, calves, knees. Two good legs wrapped around a pair of rocking hips. You have to develop a hook if you want to do the same with one. Our Father, what a disgrace, hallowed be Thy Shame. One Emperor. Seven Kings. Twenty-four Dukes. Thirteen demons who hold the rank of marquis. Ten Counts. Eleven Presidents. Xilka, Xilka, Besa, Besa.

When a person no longer has the patience to be reasonable, he must have compensating faith. Or else. Palas aron azinomas. And a few metres. Nahemah. And a few centimetres. Hand of Glory. And my leg's gone rolling down the track—without pain, miracle of miracles. The shock. Must be the shock. Hurry! Crawl after it. It must be dried and steeped in salts. And the flies leave the fish-head at last, the scent of a meatier larval bed. But, oh you foolish man! You silly goose! You're on the wrong track! Again. You've gone off the rails. One more time.

—

And so all that time I'd been on the wrong track. I lay there stunned, clutching the gravel in my bleeding hands, watching the train thunder by. The rail shook beneath my thigh and the flesh quivered mightily. Boom boom. After the train had passed, everything became perfectly clear. All the shredded paper had fallen; all the secrets disgorged and safe forever. The truck lowered its hydraulic lift and drove away. I returned to the hotel for a good night's rest, collapsing on to the bed.

—

April 4th

There's no need to worry though. This time I'll get it right. I've positioned myself on the crossing between one set of tracks and the other—where the main line splits off into one of those spurs that seem to lead nowhere now that the factories have been torn down. Or become squatter hovels. Cat-tails hide most of my body. Another train will pass in a matter of minutes—a passenger train according to the schedule. Ah, witnesses. I make sure I'm on the right track. I must admit, however, to the same fear that caused me to roll over when the axe was about to come down. I waited it out last night, but was that because I knew the train would be on the other track? Somehow had it telegraphed that message to me? Through the rail?

It doesn't matter in the long run. The day is soft and pastel-coloured. The late-afternoon clouds aren't yet in the sky. I thirst for a glass of bitter lemon. The thirst is so great it blots out everything else. A whistle. The second train is almost upon me when the signal switch shifts and catches my foot between one rail and the next. I struggle like a rabbit in a snare, bouncing in the clammy air.

I rise up in warning.

I wave my arms.

I open wide my eyes.

I piss and shit myself.

But it's too late.

I scream; the seagulls scream; the train screams.

Now, I'll never know.

Never know for sure if I could've done it on my own.

—

The first thing I did (or remember doing) when I awoke—awoke fully that is, for judging from my familiarity with my surroundings I had been awake before—was to complain about an itch in my left leg just below the knee. The doctor assured me it was a normal reaction and nothing to worry about. I reached down between the sheets, the urge to scratch intensifying as I moved closer to the spot.

The doctor sat down beside the bed and continued to talk: "There are some questions we'd like to ask you. Nothing difficult. Just routine stuff. Are you up to it?" I nodded. "Good. First of all, we didn't find any identification papers on you. What's your name?" I shrugged. "You must have a name. How else are we going to notify your family? You do have a family, don't you?" I shook my head and felt the cavity, the empty space, below my knee where the pyjamas were pinned together. My heart leaped with joy. I must've smiled.

"Well, I'm glad to see you're feeling better but surely there's someone somewhere you'd like us to contact. After all, they might be extremely worried about you, might be at their wits' end. How would you like it if someone close to you disappeared without a trace? Don't you have any feelings at all?"

I shrugged.

The itch returned, shifting from place to place within the same general vicinity. It felt a bit like a mosquito bite. Which might have been very possible as the area beneath the bridge swarmed with them. Several times, my fingers passed right through the spot without relief of any kind. I thought of sympathetic magic and my partner somewhere, squatting on the toilet perhaps jabbing at a crude image with a hair pin. Or picking up a twenty-dollar bill between her buttocks.

The doctor looked at me with large doe-like eyes, eyes of compassion and sensitivity to suffering, developed through years of practice. I felt sorry for her. Especially as she seemed so sincere. I must do my best to help her out, I said to myself.

"There is one person I'd like to see," I whispered.

"Who?" she asked, eagerly holding out the required forms.

Well, I don't exactly know her name. People call her the Prophet. But I guess, technically, that should be the Prophetess. Or is it like poet, good for both sexes? For all sexes? Her address then? Sorry, can't help you with that either as I never asked her. Didn't seem important at the time. But she should be real easy to spot because she's blind and has a thin white beard—a bunch of hairs really—and likes to slurp chicken noodle soup that she gets all over herself and she hangs out in front of this building with no windows and wherever she goes she spills sand and …

The doctor stood up, tore up the forms and walked out, announcing as she left that the healing was coming along well and that, all things being equal, I would be discharged after a month of intensive therapy.

I summoned the nurse to complain that the itch was becoming too much for even me to bear. He (female doctors and male nurses, would I ever get used to them?) pulled off the covers and had me sit up. Then, he knelt down before me and began to rub my stump. I smiled and looked around. The other three patients in the ward—all faking illness, by the way—turned away angrily and raised the volume on their TV sets. Pure jealousy on their part. I had a task; they were just floundering, useless, waiting to die.

The nurse rubbed me harder and harder till he was wringing the pyjama cloth between his hands and, to tell the truth, becoming quite excited. I knew, having seen that look of intense concentration quite often on my partner in the early days of our relationship. The halcyon days, I like to call them, when we provided our own bounce to springless mattresses. Or maybe it was just a case of transference.

"It's all in your mind," he said, breaking away reluctantly after one last squeeze. "The ghost limb effect. And you'll have to get used to it. Now, stand up and let me take you for a little walk. Soon, you'll be transferred to the convalescence wing and have your own physical therapist to help you get back on your feet again. Won't that be nice?"

"Yes, but I bet you'll miss my stump, won't you?" I said, lifting it up and wiggling it in his face. He laughed. I'd made a joke. My natural good humour was returning.

Although the itch vanished when I was fitted with my new prosthesis, the leg felt extremely uncomfortable, as if the yoking of flesh and metal hadn't quite come off. I had to lean on the therapist for balance and it was a chore walking back and forth along the corridors or on the paths of the well-manicured garden where others—some missing legs, others both arms and legs—bemoaned their fates and carried bowls around their necks to catch the falling tears. Or maybe they were practising for when they had to get out and earn a living again.

I began to grow impatient as the days passed. An impatient patient. Anything could happen in the six months between the "accident" and my scheduled release from the hospital. But nothing frightened me more than the possibility that the News Vendor had perniciously died to spite me or had decided to retire to a house by the sea, leaving his stand in the care of a healthy, two-legged youth with blue eyes and tousled hair and a dream of expanding to porn videos. The thought of the newsstand no longer existing was too cruel to be considered.

I demanded to know why I'd been kept for so long. Had they been experimenting on me? I'd heard of such things. Wouldn't put it past them. The doctor frowned (there had been a time when she smiled quite a lot) and patiently explained the reason for the delay had been because they'd done their best to save my leg. In fact, not more than two hours after the train had sliced it off, surgeons were at work trying to re-connect it, using the latest methods in micro-surgery to attach nerve on nerve, vein on vein, muscle on muscle. But the leg had only lasted a week before atrophying. A second amputation was needed and yes, in the long run, their efforts had served simply to delay my recovery.

"What did you do with the leg?" I asked. Out of curiosity, you understand.

"Your leg? Disposed of it, of course."

That was a relief. There's no telling what would've happened if my partner had got a hold of it. Or, heaven forbid, my friend, the blind Prophet(ess). Hung up somewhere like a prosciutto or an object of worship.

During my last week at the hospital, the nurse came in to tell me I had a visitor. A visitor? But that was impossible. No one knew I was there. Well, someone obviously does. She was an old, wizened lady with wispy patches of hair who mistook me for her son. Obviously a crackpot but I decided to play along with her. Especially after she brought me a bouquet of wild flowers and a box of chocolates with cherry centres.

When she first came in, she sat quietly on the edge of the bed, simply staring at me like I was some miracle or other. Then she began to talk. She talked about the kind of child I'd been, always getting into trouble and giving her plenty of reason to cry. But I wasn't bad for all that. I had a good heart. Just mischievous. She patted where my leg should've been. Remember the time, she said, you were almost run over by a car, had darted across the street without looking. I nodded, hoping she'd go on. The driver had rushed out of his vehicle, shaking and white-knuckled. Had knelt down and looked under the wheels for fear you were trapped there. And all the time you were already across the street, sitting on the curb and trembling like a rabbit.

She was a good story-teller (probably where I'd got it from) because I could see myself, the very image of a rabbit, pink eyes darting left and right and nose twitching with fear. She took the flowers and what was left of the chocolates when she left but promised to be back the next day with more stories of my youth. I looked forward to seeing her but didn't really believe she meant it.

I was wrong. She did return. She burst in on me and slapped the flowers across my face and spilled the chocolates on the bed and demanded to know—all the while in tears—why I had pretended to be her son. She couldn't be fooled, she sneered. Not by a nincompoop like me.

"But I sure fooled you," she crowed, laughing diabolically. "Yesterday, I tested you out by changing some of the details in my story. Ha, ha. My son never rolled out from under that car. He had his head crushed under that car—like a walnut. Splat! If you didn't know that, then you can't obviously be him."

I had to agree. Her logic made perfect sense. But was sad to see her leave anyway. Somehow, I got the impression she would have made a good mother.

On my final day in the hospital, the doctor came in to examine me for the last time. She still wanted to know my name. Look, she said. You don't have to tell me but we need it for health insurance purposes. I tell you what. Just write it down on the form and place it in an envelope. I won't even look at it. That's a promise. That seemed fair enough. Only one problem. Should I write my old name or the new one I'd soon have? The new one made more sense. So I wrote it down and sealed the envelope. The doctor shook my hand and wished me luck.

Later in the day, the nurse brought me two bags and placed them by the side of the bed. He told me there were two sets of clothing— one that I had been found in and some brand-new ones still in their original wrappings. He pulled them out for me. You can imagine my surprise when I saw the checkered red-and-green wool shirt and brown corduroy pants. Nice, the nurse said. But it was when he emptied the other bag that my heart truly skipped a beat. We had these cleaned and pressed. You wouldn't have thought they were once covered in blood. There, in the midst of the type of ordinary clothing that I made sure to wear in an effort to remain anonymous, were the black panties.

I hugged them, rubbed them on my face, kissed them tenderly. Don't look at me that way, I said when I saw the nurse looking at me that way. They're just a little memento mori. A remembrance of wrongs done. So help me get them on, will you? He did, slipping them over one knee and then over the stump. I felt better already. Like a new man. Just one last thing to make it a perfect day—a straight razor.

"No, I'm sorry. Those aren't allowed. Strict rules. You'd be surprised how many patients kill themselves just before they're to be released."

I assured him I had no intention of doing away with myself and we settled on a regular razor. I clipped my hair as short as possible, then sprayed the cool shaving cream evenly over my scalp. The nurse held a small mirror in front of me as I drew back the razor.

III.

I hurry through the streets towards the hotel, kicking aside discarded Halloween masks and streamers, my heart thumping, fearful that during my time away things have changed forever. That, while I was in the hospital, the News Vendor passed away or sold the stand or simply abandoned it. That I have missed the golden knock of opportunity on my door. But that fear vanishes the moment I turn the corner and catch a glimpse of him in his familiar spot, on his familiar stool. And The Hungry Artist curled up as always against the cold, covered by pieces of a cardboard box, "property of the Schloss Corp." stencilled on it. And the neon light from the hotel buzzing and struggling to stay on. I lean against the nearest wall, catching my breath. Thank God. Goddess. Or whoever is looking after me.

With a deep sigh as if he's giving away one of his own children, the Vendor hands over a newspaper to the only customer in sight and then reaches back to continue his own reading. To make sure he doesn't see me (else he might think I'm travestying him with my incomplete disguise), I skirt around to the back of the hotel, past the heaps of discarded bone and gristle piled in plastic cans behind the butcher-shop, yellow plastic cans leaking pools of blood that teem with maggots. Soon the truck will come by with its power shovel and the juices dripping down its sides. Render unto death, oh Lord.

A large dog, both paws up on a can, is trying desperately to get the top off. It manages to knock the can to the ground, then turns and snarls at me, baring its yellow teeth. There's foam on its mouth. I give it plenty of leeway and move on. Soon, I keep telling myself, it'll all be over. Not even the discomfort of walking, my imbalanced canter, can detract from a growing sense of elation.

It's an elation that's obviously not shared by the assistant manager. He collars me the moment I step inside the hotel. I smile at him as he brings his face close to mine and demands his money. What money? For the rent, of course. You think I've forgotten. There was a week's rent owing on your room when you disappeared, he says. When you skipped out. I pull out the remainder of my four hundred dollars and give it to him without bothering to count it. Here, I say. Soon, I won't be needing it. *He* counts it.

That'll do, he says, waving the money in my face before stuffing it into his back pocket. For now. However, any more tricks of that nature—or any other nature—will result in a call to the police. Is that clear? I nod. He says he's not a nasty man by nature. Just doing his duty. And to show there were no hard feelings, he allows me to have my old room back. Just make sure you have the week's rent when I come looking for it, he says. Not a problem, I say. Money is no object. I straighten up, take a breath and climb up the stairs as smoothly as possible, not wanting the assistant manager to see me limp. Not yet anyway.

But, instead of going to my third-story room, I stop in front of the room one floor below it. I'm prepared to jimmy the door open but, trusting soul, it isn't locked. I step in. The rocking-chair is moving gently back and forth in the breeze while the flowers quiver. I reach out to touch one of them. They're real! Not plastic at all. But exceedingly waxy in appearance. Almost as if a deliberate attempt had been made to disguise them. I empty a glass of water—lined with dried toothpaste—into the Javel-bottle vase and then take my place in the rocking-chair.

On one wall hangs a picture of the Blessed Virgin. She's at the foot of the Cross, looking up in anguish and acceptance. I marvel at how young she looks for a woman with a thirty-three-year-old son. Such a clear complexion! But, of course, she didn't have to suffer the rigors of childbirth. Not really. He'd just popped out. Hadn't he? Or the rigors that came before. And he didn't need much weaning either. Kinda simply raised himself, without much help from mom and dad. Candles of every shape and size surround her on an improvised altar. I light them one at a time and watch them flicker, all the while thinking: If any goes out, I'll just leave.

Down on the street, the News Vendor rushes about. This is the busiest time of day for him as hard-working and seemingly tireless people line up to discover what the world has been up to while they were busy earning a living. Okay, okay, so maybe two elderly couples are in front of the newsstand and showing interest. Nevertheless, the News Vendor makes them wait as if he's extremely busy. Good on you, I whisper.

—

As it turned out, stealing the News Vendor's wooden leg required little of the planning I'd put into it. That was disappointing. It had been my intention to divert the News Vendor with a little fire perhaps in the midst of his precious European magazine section. While he battled to put it out, I could easily spirit away his leg, stashing it under my coat. I wasn't too worried about his stand catching fire since the European magazines were isolated, aloof, on a little metal display of their own.

If I decided the Europeans were too close to the others, I could always entice—with money or candy—one of the many street urchins to steal a comic of his choice and then run. The leg would be easy prey. But today of all days there was a crowd milling about the stand—a gaggle of tourists just disgorged from a tour bus with no intention of purchasing anything and with their eyes fixed on their cell phones. And that made it possible to use a much simpler stratagem. No fire; no theft. I mingled among them, scanning the vast array of newspapers and magazines that made my heart jump with anticipation.

The News Vendor was much too busy vainly trying to convince the tourists they needed maps and tour guides of the city ("no, no, thank you, Google all I need") to notice me squat down to admire a glossy beauty close to his leg. The fact he could see no reason why anyone would want to steal the leg was another plus in my favour. With one fluid motion, acquired when short of cash in second-hand book shops and sports stores, I slid the leg beneath my coat and stood up. For a moment I considered buying the magazine I'd pretended to admire but then thought better of it. After all, one shouldn't buy things under false pretences and besides I didn't want to run the risk of having the News Vendor inspect me too closely.

—

The aluminium leg fitted by the hospital falls to the floor. I roll it into one of the Jean Louis-Lebris sacks stacked in a corner. My hands tremble like those of a man reaching out for his love for the first time as I examine the gnarled wooden peg-leg. It is unique, dotted with a series of asymmetrical holes. I pass the pads of my fingers along those empty spaces. Some are sharp—compass points; others more rounded and smooth—termites perhaps like I first surmised. I fit it slowly against my stump and strap it into place. Snug. As if it has always belonged.

My first steps are tentative, uncertain. But, before long, I am walking majestically across the room, back and forth, back and forth, admiring myself before the mirror and whispering orders to the minions below. I spin on the leg, placing all my weight on it. The worn metal cap at the bottom takes it all without a groan. Then, I practice the peculiar limp that I admired so much in the News Vendor. Just as I thought, it's the leg that does it, that makes it easy. In order not to miss the Vendor's reaction when he discovers the leg missing (for the second time), I station myself at his window and watch the crowd thinning away.

This is the happiest moment of the day for him: his stand not yet shut and the single light over his shoulder allowing him to read, God in his/her heaven and all fine with the world, the knowledge now spreading like a virus through the city, running like a common thread through each person. And knowing that he's responsible for that, for providing the cultural needle, however contaminated and largely ineffective. Soon, I tell myself, those feelings will be mine to do with as I please, to boast about them, to deny them, to falsify them, to sell them to others if I so desire. At least, that's the way it should be. Whether it's still true or has ever been true … I leave that to others to determine … the glib commentators on trends and outliers.

—

Not only were his feelings mine but his routine as well. I threw the sack over my shoulder and limped down the hotel stairs. It was heavy but manageable. The assistant manager, talking to a friend, glanced up and smiled.

"So you found it?" he asked. "I told you not to worry, that it would show up. I'm telling you though, if you don't want to have fits every time you misplace it, get yourself a spare one. And keep it in a safe place."

I thanked him for the advice. The sailor cap slipped to the side. I reached up and pushed it more firmly against my head.

"Heavy load tonight, eh?"

I nodded. The assistant manager turned away and resumed the conversation with his friend. They were holding hands across the hotel counter. Ah, love. Settles in the most peculiar of places. Outside, a pre-Christmas sale was taking place. Crowds milled about the department stores and the music blared from several loudspeakers used for advertising purposes. Two teenage girls sharing earbuds attached to a cell phone danced to their own beat, their faces expressionless, ready to be surprised by life. Soon, they were joined by others to clog up the sidewalk.

I moved on to the street. Some oldsters hailed me and asked how business was. Let's hope for an upswing, eh? My heart glowed with warmth at the concern and solicitude, at being one of the community. One gentleman—and he was obviously a gentleman with a bowler hat and a gold-headed walking stick—came jauntily out of the pool hall and offered to carry my load for me. I'm going that way, he said. Let me give you a hand. I told him that wouldn't be necessary, that I had handled heavier loads before. Further down the street, the Prophet(ess) shouted at the top of her lungs and spun in a circle, scattering sand. No one paid any attention. Surprise, surprise. I stopped in front of The Hungry Artist and dropped a coin into his tin cup. Who are you? he said. You're not him. I laughed—"quite the joker"—and walked on.

The refurbished Absinthe A-Go-Go was frenetic with activity. Long lines of perfumed and well-dressed couples fretted to get in, to catch the shows that now featured simulated sex. Some were trying to slip the doorman bribes—he took them all democratically. Others were nonchalant, acting as if they weren't really that interested in getting in. They usually made it in first. One of the girls who had once come to the apartment to pick up my partner danced topless in the new display window high above the street. I thought about my partner for a moment and felt sorry—last I heard, she'd been relegated to one of the side stages. That's what happens when one is careless about one's assets.

Within minutes, we were crossing the railroad tracks. Crossing at what seemed the exact same spot where the "accident" had taken place. I stood there for a second just to see if any of the pain had remained. Nothing but rising clouds of mosquitoes. We continued walking. At first, the gentleman's presence had me worried. But then I decided (unable to shake him anyway) that he could help me after all. We walked beneath the bridge, careful not to slip into the marshy oil-stained water with all the colours of the rainbow. On occasion, my peg-leg would sink into the ooze and then "pop-suck" when I pulled it out again. It was a satisfying sound.

We appropriated the row-boat—my row-boat now—and quickly manoeuvred to the centre of the scummy water. This is it, I said. It's deep enough here. The crickets were deafening as they rubbed their legs together; the lights of the city … the lights were all around us like fire-flies, glittering, going on and off. Lovely, isn't it? the gentleman said, scanning the horizon with his cane. Hold on, I said. He steadied the boat while I pushed the sack overboard and watched it disappear in a series of quick bubbles. And that's that, I said, dipping my hands in the water and rubbing them together. Another pile of old news gone. Bring on the new.

After he refused a generous tip for his help, I insisted on inviting the gentleman up to the room. Out of politeness, I had him sit in the rocking-chair—*my* rocking-chair—while I poised myself on the edge of the window. The invitation turned out to be a mistake. He was a deplorable talker, one who quickly shot his bolt and then was silent, irritably silent. But I still wanted someone to talk to, so I took over, reciting my life history. I began, naturally enough, with my childhood, how I'd almost been run over by a car and the wonderful inscrutable mother I had. Mother! Suddenly, I flared up and ordered him out of my chair. He jumped up, setting the chair to furious rocking, and backed away towards the door.

"You're not going to molest me," he said in a terribly fearful voice. "I don't like being molested, you know. I've never liked it—no matter what the talk on the street may be."

I apologized for my anger, explaining how I hated throwing out newspapers, even if some of the dailies were more than a week old. He suggested I hold on to them, maybe sell them for some purpose other than to be read. What! I said. My papers and magazines used to line bird cages! My papers and magazines used to hold tomato plant seedlings! Cat litter! Never! Best to dump them.

He agreed shakily. I had him sit on the bed while I took his place in the chair. Then, staring out the window at my newsstand, I continued the recitation.

"I was a proper young man, I'll have you know, a conscientious young man who worked in a process cheese factory till one day, while cleaning out the bowels of a mixing vat, its blades suddenly started up. Some people laugh at me for loving my mother. But I laugh right back because I know that, secretly, down-deep, in their hearts of hearts, they love theirs too. Did you know she came to see me? Brought me a whole mess of flowers and cherry-filled chocolates and planted a big wet kiss on my forehead. I told her all that was left to me now was to poke out an eye and become a sailor. But she said not to be silly. The days of the one-legged sailor lording it over both captain and crew are gone. They don't allow you near a ship unless you have all four limbs and two good eyes. I paid her no heed. And I did manage, on my one and only trip before my wooden leg was discovered, to make it to the Sargasso Sea where we hunted the common eel. Have you ever hunted the common eel?"

In my reverie, I didn't notice that, at some point, he'd taken the opportunity to slip out. But that didn't prevent me from talking to myself till I had the entire history unravelled, had it down pat and could recite it without hesitation. Besides, I was too excited to sleep. I unstrapped the leg and leaned it against the window so that I could support my chin on it, left elbow on the sill. In no time, I'd be circling the newsstand, picking up those neglected pieces of paper, fitting the wrong key into the lock, placing my leg against the counter. No, no. I wouldn't make the same mistake as my predecessor. My leg would be chained to the stand, one of those bicycle chains made of titanium or some such material. Anyone trying to steal it would have to drag the entire stand with him.

Inside, the ink would seep into me, blacken my face and hands. I would sit on the tiny stool and wait for my first customer. The morning would be thick with mist, swirling eddies from the bay. The people would float by like wraiths, unreal, barely alive. As all humans are before being filled with knowledge, with the facts. I would have plenty of time to scan the newspapers, perhaps even to unlock the inner chamber and to look inside.

—

The News Vendor suddenly writhes in a fit of despair. He has just noticed that his leg is gone. Frantic, wild-eyed, he searches beneath the papers, under the stand, around the sides. My partner, wrapped in a red plastic raincoat and little else, makes her way to work. Her high heels click on the sidewalk. Here I am, I whisper. Yoo hoo. I draw back as the Vendor glances up at the window. Aha, he's think-ing that he has forgotten the leg up here, that he has absentmindedly left it behind. It's a possibility, I'll grant him that.

He hops about, hurrying to close the stand. He's so concerned he doesn't bother with the ritual. That won't do, I tell myself. That's not very professional. After all, a ritual is a ritual. I lose sight of him as he bounces along the windowless building, trying to keep his balance, and then disappears into the hotel.

I hurry to dress: red-and-green checkered shirt, sailor cap, brown baggy corduroy pants held up with yellow plastic electrical cord. I mark my forehead with symmetrical fake scars and welts. (They'll be real soon enough.) And my eyes are already grey. Then I turn the chair towards the door and sit in it, rocking comfortably. The candles before the Virgin flicker but don't go out. I look up at the painting. Is it my imagination or has Mary come closer to the cross? Is she near to touching her son's foot, held in place by what resembles a railroad spike? Ah, an anomaly—like wrist watches on Centurions. And telephone poles lining Calvary.

He's hopping up the stairs now, struggling up the stairs. That must be tiring. I get up to empty one of the sacks he's filled with old, unsold papers. The papers topple over, slide across the room. Ragged piles of information. Repeated over and over. Good old Gutenberg. Father of simulacra. Bless you. I take my seat again. He's rushing towards the door, leaning perhaps against one of the corri-dor walls because, in his hurry, he's finally lost all sense of balance.

My calm, my composure has never been better. Never been more at the forefront.

He bursts into the room, flinging open wide the door so that it slams and rattles the paintings—and stops bleached in his tracks. Or track, to be precise. He tries to say something, to open his mouth. But nothing comes. Not even a tiny gasp. I stand up to greet him, hold out my arms, marvelling at the similarity between us ("You'd think we were mirror images") and complimenting him on a fine disguise. He again tries to speak, mouth opening and closing like a fish out of water, eye popping open in surprise—and totters to one side, already clutching at his chest and shuddering grotesquely before kicking out one last time and stiffening. His eyes remain open; his mouth forms a final rictus.

It's his clothes I want. Mine are good but not perfect. A foul smell fills the air. Ah, the loosening before death, the terrible loss of control, the bubbling swamp. I tell him I know what that's like. I wrap my arms around him and sit him up, prop him up against the bed. I start to undress him ever so slowly ever so gently.

There's a grimace on his face, frozen in place. He's staring at me. I reach in and close his eye lids. Outside, a party's beginning. And the street's again filling with frantic shoppers. I grab another sack from the corner pile, slip it over his head and struggle to pull it down to his feet. Then tie the end shut. Lucky he chose to die, I tell myself. It would've been a pity to have to kill him. I make sure to blow out the candles before leaving.

—

November 2nd

There's nothing like the first time, the first morning. The assistant manager's asleep at the counter when I go out into the street. Obviously, the overnight love tryst went well. The sun's not up yet and it's chilly, the steam rising from the spongy ground. There is a great deal of discarded paper on the street, so much so The Hungry Artist is practically covered. Strangely, however, the space directly in front of the stand is empty. There has not been a delivery. I make a note to myself to call later and lodge a complaint.

But right now, I have more important things to do. With tender loving care, I perform the ritual, making sure to do it exactly the way my predecessor showed me, and then unlock the stand—*my* stand. Mine and mine alone. It exhales a welcome as if it has been expecting me. Hoping for a saviour, perhaps. Someone to pull it out of its long decline.

From now on, I'll choose the newspapers, the magazines, the trinkets I want to sell; from now on, I'll make all the decisions—be they important or trivial. I sit on the stool and look around, savouring it all, enjoying the pure creation of it, the making it happen just the way I want it to. Look at me, ma. I'm an entrepreneur!

I sit all day on my stool, looking down, preparing to smile at potential customers. Where are the potential customers? I have but one: a young boy looking for the latest *Killmonger* comic. The Prophet(ess) wanders by, stops, gives the stand a good sniff, shakes her head, and continues into the alley. The Hungry Artist shambles over and holds out a bone-y hand while staring hard into my face. I drop a coin into his hand. He bows before me, whispers: "I was once on a trapeze, you know, and I know who you are," before returning to squat in his usual spot at the corner of the windowless building.

And thus the first day passes.

Before going to my room, I ask the assistant manager if I might be allowed to use the phone. Local call only, he says. Local call only, I say. He nods and points to the phone. Dial nine first. I thank him, dial nine and put in a call to the newspaper and magazine distributor. A disembodied voice, sounding either Chinese or perhaps South Asian, invites me to leave a message. In no uncertain terms, I let them know my displeasure at not having received the agreed-upon delivery. And I read out the relevant sections from the agreement between the distributor and the News Vendor.

—

The following morning, despite my vehement complaint and precise citing of the contract, which I take to be mutually binding, there again are no bundles of fresh papers and magazines waiting for me to slice open and place in the stand. But, at least this time there's a note tacked to the door of the stand. Good, I say, an explanation. That it is, of sorts:

> *Please be informed that all deliveries to newsstands in general an• your newsstan• in particular have been suspen•e• in•efinitely while Schloss Distributors undergoes fundamental re-structuring to make it more viable in the digital age. We fully realize the inconvenience this causes our clients, especially as Schloss is the last distributor of its kind following the collapse of the JK Distribution Network earlier in the year. Please also be informed that, as the newsstand is the property of a numbered holding company headquartered in Prague and controlled at arm's length by Schloss, and as it is the last of its kind, we fully intend to preserve it (following an agreement with the city museum). We trust you will take this as good news and will do your best to keep the stand in pristine shape for the future. As we coul• not fin• an email a••ress to which to sen• this note, please accept this as the 24-hour notice. Further, on the plus side, stay tuned for our streaming services. Coming soon to a device near you. As a value• ex-franchisee of the firm, we will be offering you a substantial •iscount on the first six-month subscription. Just use the following code:* Les Mouches.

I stumble about, fall against the door. I take deep breaths, hoping to hold off what I fear is an anxiety attack that would leave me helpless. Something I haven't had since high school recess. Breathe in, breathe out, breathe in. Tell yourself everything is fine. I look around. Yes! Everything *is* fine. I still have newspapers, tabloids, magazines, comics, maps, guides, knick knacks, cute gifts to sell. The stand is nearly full, packed with goodies.

That calms me down somewhat. Live for today and tomorrow will take care of itself. Make the moment count. Put on that smiley face. Carry on, carry on, carry on. Hey, you never know. Maybe, if I sell enough they'll change their minds. Yeah! Come on! Come and get it!

And it works! Suddenly, without warning, the customers start to pour in, coming from around the windowless building in waves. In grey colourless waves. Or are they coming from inside the building? Troops of lawyers and bankers and accountants. I spend the morning selling paper after paper, listening to the sound of the cash register. No time to feel sorry for myself. No time to worry about the fact my stock is being depleted very quickly, with little hope of replenishing it.

And the afternoon is the same. Magazine after magazine, comic after comic, map after map, guide after guide, fuzzy dice after fuzzy dice. It's a frenzy of buying. So much so, two of the customers (weirdly faceless in their shadowy grey selves) almost come to blows as each grabs one end of a *Superman* comic and pulls, splitting it in two. Fortunately, both had already paid for it.

At the end of the day, the newsstand is empty—like a stripped-clean carcass. All the receptacles are bare. All the little stands within the stand exposing their hooks. One last customer makes an offer on my wooden leg, an extravagant offer. I tell him to get out. The leg isn't for sale. He insists and is about to become belligerent—until the Prophet(ess) comes out of the alley spouting the thunder and wrath of the goddess and the customer has the sense to flee. The Prophet(ess) stops before the stand, feels the empty slots where the merchandise of knowledge used to be.

Ah, I see—metaphorically, of course—that you've sold it all, she says. Why? Why did you do it?

For Art's sake, I say and point to the sign across the front of the stand, forgetting for a moment that the one before me is sightless. Just for Art's sake, I repeat, liking the sound of it.

And now? she asks, the last of the sand slipping from her bags as she moves away towards The Hungry Artist, whom she'll harangue as if he were just another ordinary citizen. What will you do now?

I shrug.

What indeed will I do? I look around, feel the desolation that comes from having nothing left to sell, the emptiness in the pit of the stomach that comes from a loss of purpose. A being with nothing to look forward to. In front of an impenetrable law building. On a boat with two broken oars. And then I remember: the second key to the second doorway. I smile. Maybe not all is lost.

Nervously, my hand shaking so much I need the other one to hold it still, I fit the key in the inner chamber lock and turn it. The door springs open, almost as if in relief at being released. I peer in. With no sunlight to strike it, it's dark in there. So dark I can't make out the walls. So dark it gives the illusion of going on forever, of merging with the windowless building which I imagine is also dark and endless, primeval in its bubbling uncreative force, legal-financial-commercial files and ledgers lined up in virtual array, ready to complete their conquest; files and ledgers only super-human AI computer-robots can access properly.

And in the distance, is that the sound of a truck coming ever closer?

Now or never! I hold my breath and reach in gingerly, afraid perhaps of disappointment, of more emptiness. But, to my relief, I quickly encounter something. Not an empty space, thank goodness. Not a void to be avoided if at all avoidable. My first touch feels like a typewriter key. It *is* a typewriter key: the "Q" I bet. Even in the dark, I know immediately what kind of typewriter it is. Solid, dark and straight-backed, dignified and poised. And already clacking away. How thoughtful, I think. How appropriate. Then I touch something cool and smooth with little bumps on it. A piece of paper. The typewriter is spewing out papers, tossing them into the air as if some very powerful hand were turning the knob. Holding my breath once more, I reach in again and pull out a sheet. It appears in the pre-dusk light like a miracle ... like an impossibility.

Typed across that first page are the words: "Welcome. My name is—was—Cully. Arthur Cully. That's Cully with a 'C' but pronounced like a 'K'. So I guess you'd better call yourself Sully. Keep the first name. Or choose your own. I don't care."

Delighted, I put the page aside, place it face down on one of the empty receptacles that recently held newspapers. Then reach for another.

On the second: "The old man was thin and gaunt with deep wrinkles ..." And below: "These flies in Argos are much more sociable than its townsfolk. Just look at them!"

On the third: "Well, maybe I'm Sully and you're Cully." And below: "You have better things to do than reigning over a dead-and-alive city, a carrion city plagued by flies."

On the fourth: "Notes On The Behaviour of The Observer of Cully (Or Sully), The News Vendor, As Diligently Compiled Between March Eighth and Twentieth." And below: "They were watching him with their positively tormented faces—their skulls looked as if they had been beaten flat on top, and their features had contorted into an expression of pain in the process—they were watching him with their thicklipped mouths open, and yet not watching either, for sometimes their eyes wandered, lingering for a long time on some ordinary object before returning to him."

On the fifth: "Observations On The Notes On The Behaviour of The Observer ..." And below: "No sooner had he taken a few steps along the road than he saw two lights swaying in the distance. This sign of life cheered him, and he hurried towards the lights, which themselves were moving towards him."

On the sixth: "Continued Notes on Night-Time Activity." And below: "I woke up as the sun was reddening; and that was the one distinct time in my life, the strangest moment of all, when I didn't know who I was—I was far away from home, haunted and tired with travel, in a cheap hotel room I'd never seen, hearing the hiss of steam outside, and the creak of the old wood of the hotel, and footsteps upstairs, and all the sad sounds, and I looked at the cracked high ceiling and really didn't know who I was for about fifteen strange seconds. I wasn't scared; I was just somebody else, some stranger, and my whole life was a haunted life, the life of a ghost."

On the seventh: "Consequent Action Following Upon A Necessary Prelude." And below: "If people bring so much courage to this world the world has to kill them to break them, so of course it kills them. The world breaks every one and afterward many are strong at the broken places. But those that will not break it kills. It kills the very good and the very gentle and the very brave impartially. If you are none of these you can be sure it will kill you too but there will be no special hurry."

On the eighth ...

.

.

.

On the nth page in the first sheath: "Holding my breath once more, I reach in again and pull out a sheet. It appears in the pre-dusk light like a miracle ... like an impossibility."

I place it face down on top of the others—and smile.

Just as a flat-bed tow truck pulls up and, using a hook at the end of a pulley, begins to lift the newsstand into the air and then onto its back.

Do your worst, I whisper, holding on as the newsstand swings back and forth. There's an infinity where those came from.

About the Author

MICHAEL MIROLLA describes his writing as a mix of magic realism, surrealism, speculative fiction and meta-fiction. Publications include three Bressani Prize winners: the novel *Berlin* (2010); the poetry collection *The House on 14th Avenue* (2014); and the short story collection, *Lessons in Relationship Dyads* (2016). Among his other publications: *The Ballad of Martin B* (Quattro Books), a punk-inspired novella; three novels—*The Facility,* which features among other things a string of cloned Mussolinis; *The Giulio Metaphysics III*, a hybrid linked short stories-novel in 18 parts wherein a character named Giulio attempts to escape from his creator; and *Torp: The Landlord, The Husband, The Wife and The Lover,* a ménage-à-trois mystery set in 1970 Vancouver during the War Measures Act. 2017 saw the publication of the magic realist short story collection *The Photographer in Search of Death* (Exile Editions). A speculative fiction collection, *Paradise Islands & Selected Galaxies* is scheduled for 2020. The short story, "A Theory of Discontinuous Existence," was selected for *The Journey Prize Anthology*; and "The Sand Flea" was a Pushcart Prize nominee. Born in Italy, raised in Montreal, Michael now lives in Hamilton, Ontario. For more information, visit his website: https://www.michaelmirolla.com/index.html.